CW00421979

MY FATHER'S CHILD

MY FATHER'S CHILD

Marguerite Hegley

The Book Guild Ltd
Sussex, England

This book is a work of fiction. The characters and situations in this story are imaginary. No resemblance is intended between these characters and any real persons, either living or dead.

This book is sold subject to the condition that it shall not, by way of trade or otherwise, be lent, re-sold, hired out, photocopied or held in any retrieval system or otherwise circulated without the publisher's prior consent in any form of binding or cover other than that in which this is published and without a similar condition including this condition being imposed on the subsequent purchaser.

The Book Guild Ltd.
25 High Street,
Lewes, Sussex

First published 2000
© Marguerite Hegley 2000

Set in Baskerville
Typesetting by
SetSystems Ltd, Saffron Walden, Essex

Printed in Great Britain by
Bookcraft (Bath) Ltd, Avon

A catalogue record for this book is
available from the British Library

ISBN 1 85776 407 2

PROLOGUE

She felt the pain before she became fully conscious. A voice was saying, 'How are you feeling? You passed out and you've lost a lot of blood. How are you feeling dear?' Mary tried to raise her head. The nurse's voice sounded unsympathetic and Mary was ashamed of what she had done. She closed her eyes, pretending that she was dreaming. She wanted it to be dream. She had lost her baby, there was something wrong with the baby and it had to be taken away. She was afraid of the dream: Daniel's face, smiling above her and turning into the face of her father.

1

'Christabel is having a baby and . . . er . . . um, she asked if you could contribute – I mean, put something in . . .' Mary's voice trailed in confusion as the two young men regarded her with open amusement.

'Oh, Christabel wants us to put something in? What about the father? Oh Lordy, does she suspect one of us?'

Of all the offices on her collection round, this was the one Mary had dreaded the most. Three weeks after leaving school she had been excited to get a job as an office junior in an advertising agency in the West End of London. She had only been to the West End once on a shopping trip to the Oxford Street sales and now she was working there, in a posh advertising agency among people who were so sophisticated she felt conscious of her cheap clothes and North London accent. The secretaries were trendy and sure of themselves and barely acknowledged the shy, chubby, awkward girl with so little to say for herself.

Simon and Rollo were copywriters who shared an office. They were in their mid-twenties, smart, good-looking and apparently indifferent to the effect they had on girls. Simon in particular seemed to take nothing seriously and Mary often caught him laughing at her. He laughed a lot, throwing back his fine, shoulder-length blond hair. He made Mary think of a wayward, haughty horse. She amused herself by imagining him neighing and tossing back his mane, stamping metal-tipped shoes on the office floor. She often watched him; she was fascinated by him. His face now had that superior, amused look, and Mary was all confusion.

'I . . . I'll come back when you're ready,' she stammered and backed out of the room.

'Oh, but we're ready *now*,' said Simon, yelling after her: 'Come back, Mary, we promise we'll be gentle with you!'

Mary fled, blushing. Why was she so stupid? Why couldn't she say what she had meant to say? She had rehearsed it at home with her mother: 'I'm making a collection for Christabel who is leaving to have a baby.' She could say it perfectly at home.

'Why is Simon always laughing at me, Mum?' she had asked her mother. 'I suppose he thinks I'm stupid. He is so superior, so good-looking and so full of himself. I hate him.'

She decided she would leave Simon and Rollo out of the collection. She could not go back and face them. At home that evening she told her mother what had happened.

'They laughed at me again, Mum. I got everything wrong and they just laughed.'

'They're not our sort, people like that,' said her mother. 'It's easy for people with money. They can do what they like. You've got to be careful of people like that, Mary. You shouldn't encourage them.'

Mrs Palmer had married for the only time at 39. Her husband was a widower of 56 with three grown up children. Their first child, Rose, had been born nine months after their marriage. Mrs Palmer's second pregnancy had been unexpected and Mary's arrival to the 42-year-old woman more burdensome. Rose was a lively and friendly child who made the Palmers proud. Their second child was different. A quiet, undemanding baby, she was not the companion to Rose their mother had hoped she would be. Rose soon got impatient with her little sister and tired even of teasing her. Mary began reading at an early age and soon learned to seek refuge in books. Her father unwittingly encouraged this reticence.

John Palmer thought Mary was a child best left to herself and not troubled by outside influences. Both he and his wife were over-protective of their youngest child in their different ways. The uneasy result was that Rose, left to her own more gregarious devices, felt excluded, while Mary became more

4

isolated; each parent thinking the other favoured her. All three found Mary difficult without knowing why.

When Mary was nine her father died suddenly of a heart attack. Mrs Palmer wasn't one to share her feelings of grief and loneliness. It was as if she was ashamed of being left; that she had somehow been found wanting. She tried instead to make the best of things by working long hours and worrying about her two daughters, left to their own devices at home. Both girls were wary of showing their feelings, and uneasy in the world.

Rose's shock pregnancy was blamed solely on Dave, her boyfriend of only a few weeks. To Mrs Palmer's mind, her daughter would never have done such a thing and must have been deliberately plied with drink. That her pregnancy was an escape from home had occurred neither to mother nor daughter.

Mary stood clutching her third glass of wine, in a dress hastily borrowed from Rose, at the edge of Christabel's leaving party. The kindly Christabel had left after 40 minutes with her stockbroker husband and Mary had been awkwardly standing by herself for some minutes. She took a large gulp of wine, wishing she could think of something to say, while everyone else flirted and drank and hooted with laughter in their loud, confident voices.

'Come on, rabbit, said Simon's voice. She looked up at him in panic. He was laughing at her again. 'Let's go and get some air. You look as though you are about to choke.'

'I must go home,' said Mary primly. 'I didn't realise it was so late.'

'I'll take you. Come on, we'll get a taxi. Where do you live?' said Simon, ignoring her protests. Mary did not want to tell him.

'It's too far for a taxi,' she said. 'You can't . . .' She was horrified at the thought of Simon seeing the shabby terraced house in its run-down neighbourhood. He was only doing this so he could humiliate her.

5

'Come on, rabbit,' he said. 'Come on!'

He kissed her all the way home in the back of the cab. She had shamefacedly admitted to 'Tottenham' and seen his superior sneer. He did not care that the taxi driver could see them. One hand inside her dress, which he had skilfully unbuttoned, he was saying: 'You have lovely breasts. And I'm definitely in love with this one.'

She got out of the cab quickly at her front door, hoping it would go away, taking Simon with it. But he was behind her as she fumbled for her key.

'Coffee, I think,' he said.

Mary dreaded a confrontation with her mother. She did not know what to do. As she opened the front door, not daring to put on the light, Simon was right behind her in the hallway. Immediately the landing light came on and her mother was at the top of the stairs looking dishevelled and angry.

'Where have you been? I've been worried sick!' Mrs Palmer stopped when she saw Simon. She stood looking at them and then turned abruptly away. Mary was too embarrassed to look at Simon; she knew he would be smiling. She feared that any minute he would toss back his beautiful mane and laugh out loud.

He casually walked into the front room and switched on the light. Mary felt ashamed. The room was very untidy. Katie, Mary's cat, was asleep on the best armchair, which was covered in her hairs. What Mary saw through Simon's eyes was pathetic and poverty stricken and sad. But she could not ask him to go. She could only think that her mother would be angry. And she couldn't blame her. How could she have done this? Brought a stranger home to embarrass her poor mum?

Simon said, 'Where's the coffee then?' Mary felt herself redden. 'Come on, rabbit,' he said, kissing her, his hands on her breasts. He heard a noise upstairs and stopped abruptly. 'Okay, I'll go, say goodbye to your mother for me.'

When the front door had closed Mrs Palmer came down the stairs. 'Who was that? What have you been doing?'

'Nothing, Mum, it's all right,' said Mary. 'We had Christabel's do and he saw me home, that's all. Nothing happened'.

Mary managed to avoid Simon for the next few days at the office. The following Friday some of the people from the agency planned to try a new club off Oxford Street and Mary felt it would be safe to go. She felt flattered to be included. Simon would be surrounded by besotted girls and would ignore her anyway. She resigned herself to this. She was a silly working-class girl who lived in a hovel. He would be off with Felicity or Abigail; she knew he had been out with both of them. They were tall and slender with long, blonde hair and perfect legs. Next to them, Mary was chubby and her thick, curly dark hair never looked smooth, no matter how determinedly she blow-dried it. She could never manage to make up her eyes the way they did. She could not compete and would not try to. She decided it was a good thing Simon had seen her home: he would not bother with her now.

Mary bought a daring new mini-dress for the club. When she arrived home, Rose and her now husband Dave were there with their baby Marty. Mary excitedly showed them the dress and boasted that she was going to a posh club in the West End. She was going to have a good time.

'That dress is a bit tarty, and it's not your colour,' said Rose, as soon as her mother was out of earshot. 'Isn't it a bit short? It looks so common. I thought they was posh where you work.'

'It'll be hot in the club,' said Dave. 'I think it's very sexy, Mary.'

Mary said anxiously, 'You don't think I look too fat?'

'Well, you ain't thin, but you've got great tits and your legs aren't bad. Whoever you're trying to pull will be there for it,' said Dave.

'Shut up, Dave,' said Rose, in a panicky whisper. 'Don't let Mum hear you.'

But, too late, Mrs Palmer came into the room and banged the teapot down on the table so that hot tea spilled out and scalded her hand. She said nothing as Rose and Mary looked at the floor, avoiding eye contact. Dave sat back in his chair with a smirk of triumph and lit a cigarette.

Rose and Dave were both eighteen. They had been married for six months and Marty was eight weeks old. The pregnancy and rushed marriage had been a deep source of shame to Mrs Palmer and, by association, to Mary, as were Rose and Dave's struggles to make ends meet. They were often unable to pay their rent and both Mrs Palmer and Mary were called upon to help them out.

Rose loyally came to see her mum two or three times every week, proudly bringing her little boy, who was as lively and happy a baby as she herself had been. She appeared not to notice that her mother was rather grim-faced in her approval of him. She never questioned her mother. Mrs Palmer was as generous as she was able to be, while Mary felt a sense of pride, and even superiority, in helping her big sister financially. She felt her life was beginning. She was wary of making the same mistake as her sister had: by marrying someone like Dave. She was unaware that this made her appear standoffish and prim to her contemporaries.

The club-goers gathered in the pub after work. Mary sat self-consciously in her mini-dress, drinking orange juice. She was excited about her first club and amused to see the snobby secretaries vying for the attention of Simon and Rollo, who stood coolly aloof. Mary was going to enjoy herself. She had been too self-conscious to go to school dances, she had always been teased about being fat. She and Rose danced to records at home, playing them loudly when their mother was out.

She remembered being about 7 or 8 and dancing with her dad. She was being kept home from school because of measles or chicken pox or one of the frequent childhood diseases she was prey to. She remembered her dad, moving with stiff legs while her feet rested on his, waltzing her round and round the room while they both laughed.

8

She loved dancing and planned to stay on the dance floor, out of Simon's way. She saw him at the bar, talking with a French girl called Mireille who had just joined the agency. Mireille was dark-haired and mysterious-looking, not at all like the other girls. Mary felt uneasy. She noticed that Mireille was regarding Simon coolly, not hanging onto his every word and giggling as girls usually did, and she noticed that Simon was not laughing. He was looking gravely into Mireille's expressionless face. Mary felt a sudden, painful jealousy. This turned quickly into a hopeless feeling that she would never be good enough, clever enough or even simply cool enough for someone like Simon. She would always be clumsy and awkward and the Simons of this world would always be beyond her reach.

Her mother was right. It was the rich, smart and glamorous people who got what they wanted. She managed to stay clear of Simon and Mireille and enjoyed herself, drinking far more than she had ever done. She felt that at last she was beginning to make friends. She forgot the time. It occurred to her suddenly that she had probably missed the last train home. At that moment she heard Simon's voice close to her ear.

'Everyone's coming back to my place, Mary. Are you coming? Come on, you can phone your mum.' Mary looked at him blankly. 'Come on, rabbit, there's a phone in the foyer. Phone your mum.' He laughed. 'I'll speak to her if you like.'

Mrs Palmer sounded anxious. 'Whose house are you going to? Don't have anything to drink.'

'No, Mum it will be all right. I'm going to Janet's. It'll be all right,' said Mary. 'I won't be late.' Mrs Palmer put the phone down abruptly. Mary's money had run out. Outside in the street Simon hailed a taxi.

'Come on rabbit,' he said, 'the others are following in Rollo's car.'

Mary was talkative in the taxi. 'What's it like being a copywriter?' she said, not caring if it was a silly question.

'Well, I do a lot of writing apart from copywriting,' said Simon. 'I've done some work at Elstree.'

'What, films, do you mean?' said Mary.

'Scripts, they're called scripts,' said Simon impatiently. 'If not the whole script, I've been called upon to write some dialogue on occasion.'

'What famous people have you met?' Mary was eager for conversation now. Simon laughed, repeating sarcastically, almost to himself, 'Famous people'.

'All these questions,' he said loudly. 'Suddenly the rabbit can't stop talking.'

Mary was wide-eyed at Simon's flat. She had never seen such luxury – fitted carpets, leather sofas, soft lighting and a stereo.

'What sort of music do you like?'

'The Who,' said Mary, laughing. She felt relaxed and happy. She was looking forward to the others coming; it occurred to her that she could cope with people when she was a bit drunk. She was beginning to feel confident about making friends.

'Who?' said Simon, breaking into a smile.

'Why are you always laughing at me?' said Mary. Feeling her insecurity returning, she sat down suddenly on a sofa. Simon immediately sat down beside her and she stiffened.

'Oh, I've done it again, haven't I? I've frightened the little rabbit.'

Mary said nothing. Then, to hide her confusion, she blurted out, 'When are the others coming?'

Simon roared with laughter and began kissing her, slowly taking off her clothes. 'You can't,' she said. 'I can't.' Simon stood up and pulled Mary to her feet.

'Come and see the bedroom,' he said, steering her before him, a hand on one breast, the other caressing her bottom.

'Where are the others?' Mary asked. 'You said the others were coming.'

'Oh, so the rabbit wants group sex?' said Simon. 'OK, we'll wait for the others, then.'

'No, no I didn't mean . . .'

'Well, it's just you and me then,' said Simon, taking off his clothes.

Seconds later his body was pinning hers to the bed. He was kissing her and pulling her hair gently. Then not so gently, forcing her thighs apart and murmuring over and over: 'Do you want it, do you want it?' Simon's mouth was close to her ear. His voice, his beautiful blond mane brushing her face and neck, and the movement of his body, had a hypnotic effect on her. 'Do you want it, Mary? Say if you want it.'

Her body wanted him; her body was acting on its own. Her legs wrapped themselves around him. She heard her own voice say: 'Yes . . . Yeeeeeeees!'

He stopped abruptly, rolled off her and turned his back on her without speaking. She opened her mouth, but could not make a sound. What had happened? Why had he stopped? She was unable to ask him. He switched off the light without a word. She lay there numbly. She tried to tell herself she had not wanted him after all. She lied to herself. She was not like that. She did not want him. But she kept hearing her own voice over and over: 'Yes . . . Yeees!' She began to cry silently, aware that Simon made no movement or sound. Finally she fell asleep. She awoke to find him smiling at her. She tried to explain.

'I'm sorry. My sister got pregnant last year and had to get married. It nearly killed my mother.'

'Well I've heard of childbirth nearly killing the mother, but the grandmother! That's a rare biological feat,' said Simon sarcastically.

He got up and went into the kitchen, coming back with coffee for her. She looked at him imploringly. 'What did I do wrong? I'm not used to this, I told you. I explained to you,' she said helplessly.

'It's a matter of fashion.' Simon sounded bored. 'In Victorian times you would have been right to *save*' – he emphasised the word sarcastically – 'yourself. In another age you'd be a very naive young girl. Some girls want you to believe they don't want it so they don't have to take any responsibility. Maybe you're like that. Some girls want to be raped.'

Mary was shocked at the word but stayed silent. How could she confess her innocence when she had wanted him? Whatever she had thought before, when it came to it she had wanted him. And now she felt ashamed.

11

'Take Christianity,' said Simon. 'I can't help thinking that if there was a God, he'd have better representatives on earth than your average *vicar*.' He gave a contemptuous emphasis to the word. But Mary did not hear him. She was thinking about Mireille.

'Haven't you ever been in love?' she asked.

Simon snorted. 'I lived with a girl once, if that's what you mean, but never again. You never know who's around the corner.'

'Who was she?' asked Mary, thinking that perhaps it had been Mireille.

'She was just a girl, she had beautiful breasts. It lasted a week. After I left, she kept phoning me at the office. She became a nuisance. One day she said she had a lot of pills and she was going to take them all if I didn't come back. So I said, "Go ahead. Shame about your breasts, though."'

Mary was too shocked to speak. Simon was laughing again. 'Don't worry, little rabbit. She didn't do it. She's married now, the silly bitch. I see her occasionally.' he paused. 'Look, Mary, if you're going to do this you'd better get yourself on the pill. Get dressed now, and I'll get you a cab.'

She dumbly obeyed. She did not protest when he saw her to the door with the money for the cab in her hand, and she walked slowly away as he firmly closed the door behind her. She got the taxi driver to drop her just around the corner from her house, close to where her school friend, Janet, lived. She knocked on the door. Janet's Mum opened it.

'Where were you last night, Mary?' she said. 'Your mum came around at one o'clock and woke us all up, looking for you.'

Janet appeared and pulled Mary into the front room. 'Why didn't you tell me? I could've said you were here. Your mum went mad. She said you were here, and we didn't know what to say. It was one in the morning. My dad went mad. What's going on, Mary?'

How could she have forgotten her mother? Mary could not believe that she had taken such a risk. What would her mother say? Where could she say she had been?

Mrs Palmer was behind the front door. 'Where have you been until now? I've been worried *sick*. Why didn't you think of *me*? How could you tell such *lies*? Your father would wipe the floor with you!'

'Nothing Mum, I've done nothing,' was all Mary could say.

On Monday morning, after a tense weekend, Mary could not face the office. She went to see her sister Rose and told her about Simon. Rose was scathing.

'He sounds so stuck up. You were stupid going back to his flat. Anyone but you would've known what he was after, you silly cow. You could do better than him. He sounds awful.' She laughed. 'It's not that difficult, look at me and Dave.' She was cradling little Marty in her arms and kept nuzzling his neck and making little kissing noises. The baby's eyes were fixed on her face.

'But you got pregnant,' said Mary.

'Yes, but Dave married me. What would your stuck up Simon have done?'

'But he wouldn't' – she lowered her voice – '*do it*, because I wasn't on the pill.' Mary hesitated. 'Rose, can I ask you something? Are you on the pill, now?'

'Thinking about it,' said Rose. 'Um, we . . .' She shut her mouth suddenly. She had been going to say something and then changed her mind.

'How can you get it, then?'

'No, Mare, you can't. You're only sixteen. And all because some stuck up git twice your age—'

'He's not, he's twenty-six. And I'm seventeen in November', said Mary.

'Look, Mare, you forget about this. What if Mum found out? Why do you want to work up West anyway? You could get a local job. You're heading for trouble, the way you're going. Mum couldn't take any more.'

Mary phoned work from a call box and said she was on her way to the doctor because she was unwell. Not wanting to go home, she went to the local library. Reading the notices, she saw one for the local family planning clinic. Feeling like a condemned soul, she telephoned to make an appointment.

The nurse was cold and businesslike. She took Mary's details and referred constantly to 'your fiancé'. She told Mary she would have to take a smear test and her blood pressure before any contraceptive pill could be prescribed. Not knowing what a smear test was, Mary was unprepared for the pain of her first time. She wondered if the nurse had assumed she was not a virgin. She was too ashamed and traumatised to tell her. The cold steel seemed to tear at her insides and she bit her lip so hard to stop from crying out that it tore and bled. She could hear Simon's voice: 'Oh, I've frightened the little rabbit.' That's all I am, she thought, a silly, frightened rabbit. She heard no more of what the nurse was saying. She caught her look of disapproval and felt ashamed. She was glad to be out of the clinic. It was only then that she realised she had not asked what would happen next. She no longer cared. She wanted to see Simon. She wanted to explain herself to him. She just wanted a chance to explain.

For the rest of the week in the office Simon ignored her. She felt that all the people in the agency knew about her and were laughing at her. Her work suffered. She could not sleep until the early hours of the morning. She overslept and was late for work. At last, Friday evening came and she could go home, away from the daily humiliation of Simon cutting her dead. Of everyone knowing how stupid she was.

When she got home Rose and Dave were there with little Marty and all their belongings. Mrs Palmer was in the kitchen, grimly washing up. Rose told Mary that they had been asked to leave by their landlady.

Mrs Palmer came into the room. 'I was so ashamed. That common woman. She said she was glad no daughter of hers had married such a waster. What did she mean?' She did not look at Dave, addressing her remarks to Rose, who stood crying silently and hopelessly, clutching the distressed Marty.

The tension was only broken when, on Saturday afternoon, Rose and Mrs Palmer took Marty to visit Uncle Pete, Mrs Palmer's only brother, two years her junior. Mary stood at the

14

window of the boxroom watching boys playing football in the street. Since England had won the World Cup everyone seemed to have gone football mad. Dave was convinced that when Marty was old enough he'd have a trial for Spurs. He spent every Saturday in the season watching football and had become unbearable since England's win.

'Look at those legs,' he'd say. 'They're footballer's legs. They're Spurs legs.' And he would grab Marty and run him around the room, making him kick his legs until Rose pleaded with him, 'Don't, Dave, you're hurting him.'

Rose, Dave, Marty and their belongings had taken over Mary's room. As she watched the boys' game Mary was planning what she would say to Simon about the Pill. She knew if she could just speak to him it would be all right. She would tell him about the Pill, he would be pleased and it would be all right. The door opened behind her and she turned to see Dave. He was smoking a cigarette and smirking.

'Lo, Mary,' he said. 'What you up to, then?'

'Nothing,' said Mary, blushing with shame and confusion.

Dave crossed the room and stood very close to her. She could smell the cigarette smoke on his breath, and on his clothes. He stubbed the cigarette out with slow deliberation in her one treasured piece of china, a souvenir of a holiday in Devon. He came close to her again, still smirking. 'Rosie told me you're on the Pill,' he said, and laughed. 'And you always so stuck up, so high and mighty, like you never did it.' His face lurched suddenly at hers and, his hands grabbing at her breasts, he began kissing her hard on the mouth. The smell of cigarettes made her choke.

She pulled away. 'Don't, Dave, don't!'

'Oh, come on Mary, you're on the Pill, come on Mare, no harm done.'

'No, Dave. Look, I like you. Look, it's not that I don't like you. But, but Rosie, she's my sister. We can't.'

'Don't you fancy me, then? I know you do,' said Dave.

She felt her face redden. He saw through her. He knew she was no good really. He had been laughing at her. He thought she was a silly, stuck-up bitch. She started to say, 'But I'm not on the Pill yet . . .' then stopped, fearing he would think she *wanted* sex with him. She was afraid.

'Look, Dave, they might come back. Don't, Dave.'

'They won't be back yet. They've gone to Pete's. They'll be jawing all day.'

'Dave, look, it's not that I don't like you. It's Rosie, you see.'

He guffawed. 'I know you do,' he said. 'And I know it will happen one day.' He left the room. She sat down on the bed, shaking. His head came round the door.

'I'm living here, now, Mary,' he said.

2

Mary's negative smear test results arrived through the post at the end of the following week. At first she felt panic, thinking 'negative' meant there was something wrong with her. She had become completely self-obsessed: grimly getting through each day, unaware of the notice people at work were taking of this. Simon was talking to her now, but he was standoffish and cold and Mary spent a lot of her time crying in the ladies.

She made another appointment at the clinic and this time was given her pills, with the instructions that she must wait for her next period before beginning the course. When at last she was successfully taking the Pill, she went into Simon's office. This was going to make it all right. She was relieved to see that Rollo was not there. Simon looked at her with an expression of polite enquiry.

'I'm on the Pill now, Simon,' she stammered. If he had laughed she might have felt better. But his expression was cold.

'And what does this have to do with me?' he enquired.

Just then his phone rang and he picked it up. He was evidently very pleased to hear from whoever was on the end of the line, and was soon talking animatedly. With a sudden rush of jealousy, Mary thought it must be Mireille. She ran from the room. Why had she not been prepared for this? What had she expected him to say? Why, oh why was she so stupid? She remembered the girl he had lived with for a week. He wouldn't care if I took lots of pills, she thought. Oblivious to the people who stared at her, she ran into the ladies and sobbed.

Mary stayed at home the next day, saying that she was not

well. The following day she could not face the office. She phoned to say that she was going to see her doctor. After three days, her mother said she should go back to work. She seemed all right now. A shock awaited her. Susannah, the secretary to the MD, who also acted as personnel officer to the junior staff, asked to see her.

'Come in, and sit down, Mary,' she said in a kindly voice. 'Let's see, you've been with us for . . . Let's see, is it . . . eight weeks?'

It had seemed longer to Mary, but she nodded dumbly, sensing something awful was coming. 'You've done well, Mary, and everyone likes you. But we wonder if an agency is really the place for you? We wonder if perhaps you wouldn't be happier somewhere else?'

'No,' protested Mary. But she knew it was no good. She started to cry. 'What can I do?' she wailed.

'We'll give you a month's money and you can go now. No need to explain to anyone.'

Mary obediently took the money offered to her, unable to speak. She wanted to ask 'Why?' and 'Please let me see Simon,' but she sensed she should say nothing. Taking sudden pity on her, Susannah put her arm around her and walked her out of the main doors to a café on the corner of the road. She ordered coffee for Mary and then left her. Mary walked to Bond Street tube station and got on the first train. She couldn't think what to do. She'd got that job from an employment agency. How could she now go back and tell them she had been asked to leave? She had a month's money, so at least she didn't have to tell her mother yet. She travelled to the end of the Central Line and then caught a train back, travelling backwards and forwards until it was time to go home.

Dave was out of work and hanging sheepishly about the house, where an uneasy, unspoken tension was ever-present. Marty had become fretful and cried a lot at night. Rose was unable to cope with him and she and Dave could be heard rowing in loud whispers through the thin wall between their room and Mary's. With the house messier than ever, Mary was

18

glad to leave every day at 8 a.m., travelling to Bond Street tube station, as usual. She spent her days reading novels and drinking tea in cafés until it was time to go home. She was becoming less than confident about going back to the employment agency to find another job and felt intimidated when trying a different one. She had walked into one employment agency and been scared off by the professional smiles and gushy, phoney welcome. The girls there reminded her of the secretaries at her former job; the ones she knew would now be laughing at her. Mary's money was running out. She had to make each cup of tea last an hour and was spending more time staring out of the café window than reading.

Someone was speaking to her. 'I've accidentally put sugar in my tea, and I'm trying to cut down. Would you like it?'

She looked up to see a kindly-looking, middle-aged man holding out a cup and saucer to her, which she took without thinking. He sat down opposite her in a companionable silence, while she took a sip of the tea and grimaced. 'What's wrong with it?' he asked.

'It's all right, but I don't take sugar,' she said, beginning to cry. She suddenly felt very hungry and desperate.

'My name is Geoffrey Hartley,' said the man. 'What's your name?'

'Mary Palmer.'

People were beginning to look at them. Mary stood up suddenly. Mr Hartley got to his feet. 'Mary, let's go and get some good coffee.' He walked behind her out of the café. Outside it had begun to rain and Mary put on her thin raincoat, hurrying to get out of sight of those people in the café who had seen her crying.

'I'm just round the corner in Mount Street,' said Mr Hartley. 'You can have some coffee and something to eat, no charge'. She followed him without a word.

His flat was surprisingly smart for such a nondescript middle-aged man. Mary thought he looked like an absent-minded librarian. She was grateful to sit with him in his clean, functional kitchen. The coffee tasted very nice; she hadn't had real ground coffee before. They had some Danish pastries, which Mr Hartley said were his weakness. Mary had eaten three before it occurred to her that she was being very greedy.

Mr Hartley seemed not to notice. He appeared to be content to sit drinking coffee. He didn't seem to require conversation. He asked her politely if she would like some music and then put on a classical record she had never heard before. The music was very soothing. Mary sat back and felt at ease for the first time in months. She felt as she had as a small child when she listened to the radio with her dad. She remembered a winter afternoon when her dad had sat in the armchair opposite her, roasting chestnuts in the coal fire and handing them like great treasures to her, after taking off the skins.

'What do you do, Mary?' Mr Hartley's voice broke suddenly into her thoughts. It was such a kind and gentle voice that Mary, her mood shattered and reality breaking over her, began to cry again, sobbing that she had no money left to pay her mother for her keep, and no money for food or train fares.

'Look, Mary,' said Geoffrey Hartley. 'I need someone to help me here. I would pay you. You could start doing just afternoons.'

'I can't type very well,' she said. 'Er . . . oh . . . cleaning, you mean?' She had only seen the kitchen of his flat but it looked so spotless, she thought it would be easy work. 'I can't cook, or anything.'

'Mary, I'll give you some money now, so you can pay your mother your keep. You can come back on Monday at one.'

Feeling herself dismissed, Mary stood up and looked around for her coat. Mr Hartley led her to the front door and took out his wallet, pressing some notes into her hand. As Mary got outside and unfolded the notes to put them in her bag, she saw that she had been given £50. She had never seen so much money and wondered if Mr Hartley had made a mistake. She looked back at the door, wondering if she should give the money back. For a minute or two she hesitated. Then

20

she went back and knocked on the door. After a few minutes, Mr Hartley opened it.

'Er, Mr Hartley, um, you've given me too much money,' she stammered. She suddenly felt silly. Why hadn't she just taken the money and gone? She looked at Mr Hartley and wondered if it had been a sort of test of her honesty.

'No, you keep it, Mary, it's wages in advance. You can give your mother her keep. I'll see you on Monday at one o'clock.' And he gently closed the door. Mary wondered what sort of house he imagined she lived in. Fifty pounds was well over what she gave her mother for her keep.

The next day was Saturday. Mary didn't have to get up early or pretend to go to work. She bought some new eye make-up and spent hours in her room trying to get the fashionable look, copied from the secretaries in the agency. She was finally very pleased with the result. It made her look very different. Her mother said it was 'too black', but hadn't said any more. Rose had immediately asked Mary to make her eyes up, too. She and Rose had been shopping together and Mary was able to buy them coffee and cakes. She felt very happy for the first time in ages and decided to buy a new dress for work on Monday.

'You're so lucky, Mary,' said Rose. 'I wish I'd just got paid. It's awful with Dave not working. He and Mum don't hardly speak to each other now. I don't think she likes him.'

Mary stayed silent. She knew if she told Rose about Dave coming into her room she would not be believed. She asked Rose if she had mentioned the conversation they'd had about the Pill to Dave.

'Yes, I told him. He thought you were mad, too. You didn't though, did you Mare?'

'Well, I did,' she replied. 'But Simon doesn't speak to me now, so I needn't have bothered.'

'But, what's it like?' said Rose. 'Dave's on at me to go on it.'

'It can't be as bad as having a baby,' replied Mary.

When they got home Uncle Pete had just arrived. He

scarcely looked at Mary and then said to his sister: 'Why do you let her go out with all that muck on her face?'

'All the girls wear lots of eye make-up now,' said Mrs Palmer, taking the tea things into the living room.

'Well, you girls have all got the Pill, now, haven't you?' said Uncle Pete.

Mary said nothing, looking at the floor, her face reddening. Had Dave told him, or was he just saying that? Uncle Pete was speaking again, sounding angry.

'That broke your mother, your sister going off like that. She relied on you. You were the clever one. She expected you to have more sense.'

'I haven't done anything, Uncle Pete.'

He ignored her and went on: 'Going about like that. You have to think of your mother.'

Mrs Palmer came back into the kitchen. 'She never goes anywhere except work, and she likes her job. She's getting on all right. Leave her, Pete.'

Pete would not be swayed: 'You were too soft on those girls, Molly. We never did anything like that when we was kids, going about like a little tart.'

Mary left the house at the usual time on Monday morning. When she got to the station she found that she had lost the rest of the money Mr Hartley had given to her. She had some change, but that was all. Of the £50 she had been given, she'd spent just under half, including the money she had given to her mother for a month's keep. Where could she have lost it? It must have been on the way home from shopping with Rose. She'd had the money in the shop when she had paid for the dress. She remembered taking care not to let Rose see the notes in her purse.

She decided against telling Mr Hartley. She did not want him to think she could not be trusted. She would just be able to afford her fare, if she walked part of the way. It was raining when she left Holborn tube station. She had decided she would walk down Oxford Street. The rain seemed exhilarating to Mary. She was happy to be able to earn some money. Mr Hartley was such a nice, kind man. She walked aimlessly, not caring that her hair was getting curlier in the fine, misty rain.

As she found herself in Bedford Square the rain began to get heavier and she sheltered in the doorway of a house, which seemed empty. There was scaffolding outside but then she saw that the dusty door was ajar. There were dustsheets covering the floor in the hallway and the stairs. Two builders came down the stairs.

'Raining cats and dogs, luv?' said one.

She laughed. 'I must look more like a drowned rat.'

'Come in and wait till it stops,' said the younger one, who didn't look much older than Mary. 'It's time we had a tea break.'

Upstairs they found a room with some furniture and took the sheets off a large sofa so that Mary could sit down.

'Mick and Stu,' Mick said. 'What's your name?'

'What you doing out in the rain on a Monday morning, Mary?' said Stu.

'I've got a new job and I don't start until one o'clock,' she replied. 'And I like walking in the rain, anyway.'

They sat on either side of her, smiling. Then the younger one, Mick, said he would go to the café to get them all some coffee.

'How do you like it, Mary?' he asked with a wide smile.

When he had gone, Stu said, 'You're very pretty, Mary.' She laughed, feeling shy. He suddenly kissed her and it was nice. She kissed him back. 'You're hot stuff,' he said awkwardly. He kissed her again, and then began undoing the top button on her new dress. 'Your clothes are all wet. Better take them off.'

Without waiting for her reply, he pulled the mini-dress over her head and then took off her bra. He began to kiss her left breast very gently while running his fingers slowly over and around the right one. Mary closed her eyes. She thought of Simon and how she had wanted him. Stu was kissing her mouth now while taking off her tights and knickers, running his hands up and down her thighs and then up again to her breasts, saying over and over again: 'You're so pretty, Mary,

23

you're so sexy, Mary.' Mary leaned back and looked into Stu's face. He was smiling at her without embarrassment now, and she laughed.

'What you laughing at, gorgeous?' he asked good-naturedly. Not waiting for a reply, he kissed her mouth again, his fingers moving up her thighs and exploring inside her. She felt his fingers moving gently into her and tried to relax.

She did not hear Mick return. With her eyes closed she heard Simon's voice saying again and again: 'Do you want it, do you want it?'

'Yes . . . Yeeeeeeees,' she said. Her hands in Stu's hair, she was kissing him energetically, pretending it was Simon. She could feel his body against hers, she felt him enter her. She remained with her eyes closed, leaning her head back as he cupped her breasts with his hands, pushing urgently into her. She did not want to open her eyes. She knew by now that she and Stu were not alone. The idea suddenly made her laugh. She opened her eyes and raised her head. Stu was red in the face, thrusting his penis into her. She looked at Mick and smiled. Then she raised her arms to him, saying 'Come on, come on.' She hurt, her insides felt very sore. She remembered the stony-faced nurse with her cold steel and the comparison with Stu's penis made her laugh again. He finally collapsed on her with a huge sigh and said, 'Blimey you were tight, Mary.' He raised himself up and then said, 'Oh God, oh God.'

Mick stopped kissing Mary's breasts to look at his friend, then followed his horrified gaze. Blood was all over Stu's penis, Mary's thighs and the sofa.

'Why didn't you tell me, Mary?' said Stu. 'I'm sorry Mary. I didn't know. Did I hurt you, Mary, I'm sorry. It felt really good for me.'

Mick handed Mary a cup of coffee. 'Are you all right?' he said. 'You chose a funny time to lose it, girl!'

They sat for a full minute drinking their coffee.

'You can have shower, Mary,' said Mick at last. Mary nodded in agreement. She could think of nothing to say.

She let the water caress her, rubbing her hands all over her

24

body, feeling comforted and soothed. She was relieved that something that could have been so awful had not been so bad. Knowing that she would never see Stu and Mick again made it seem easier.

There were no towels dry herself on. Mary hung her clothes over the back of the sofa to dry and then sat down. 'I have to look smart today for my job.'

She realised how daft this sounded in view of what they had been doing. Mick and Stu showered and then the three of them sat together naked on the sofa, laughing. Mick got up to bolt the front door. It was raining very hard outside, beating against the windows. Mick came back into the room. 'How are you feeling, Mary?' he asked.

'I'm okay,' she said.

'Good,' said Mick. 'There are other things we can do.'

Mary looked at him in mock surprise. 'What things?' she asked.

'We can lick you,' said Stu.

'And you can lick us,' said Mick.

'And my big brother can lick your big brother' said Mary. They rolled with laughter on the sofa.

'I knew I should have got some ice cream,' said Mick.

Mary lay back on the sofa and Mick ran his penis around her mouth, teasing it open. She put out her tongue and he eased himself in, moving his penis rhythmically in and out while Stu's hands moved slowly down her stomach and between her legs, stroking her until she began to respond. He started licking her and pushing his tongue into her. His tongue felt soft and tickley and was making loud kissing noises, which made her laugh. Then he began teasing her clitoris in earnest, stroking her with his fingers, while Mick's penis grew harder and more urgent in her mouth. She began moaning and moving her body urgently. The intensity of feeling made her thrust so violently that Mick's penis hit the back of her throat, making her choke.

Mick withdrew his penis and aimed it, just in time, away from Mary's face. 'Time to decorate the ceiling,' he said as he came.

25

It was 12.30 and Mary had to leave for work.

'If you don't like your new job, you can come and work with us,' said Stu as she waved goodbye.

'Thank you for having me,' she said, laughing.

At one o'clock Mary found that Mr Hartley was not alone. He had a visitor from America. 'May I introduce Anton, who is the son of a colleague?' They shook hands and then Mr Hartley suggested lunch. Throughout the meal which, to Mary's surprise, she was not expected to make, Anton and Mr Hartley were very polite and friendly, asking Mary about her home life and the sort of food she liked. At just after two Mary said nervously, 'When do you want me to start work, Mr Hartley? Do you want me to wash up?'

'We won't start today,' he replied. 'Come back tomorrow at the same time. Do you need any more money?'

'No, I'm all right,' said Mary. She realised that she wouldn't be able to come back the next day as she didn't have the fare.

'Well, maybe my fare,' she said, feeling like a thief.

That evening was a tense one. Mrs Palmer said she had a headache and went to bed early. Mary was finding it increasingly difficult to make conversation with Dave. She was sorry that Marty was always asleep when she got home.

Mr Hartley was alone when Mary arrived the next day and he let her help with the lunch. He had another American guest he wanted her to meet. By Thursday, Mary was beginning to find it odd. Why was she meeting all these business acquaintances? The pattern was always the same. They made polite conversation and they ate lunch.

When she arrived home on Thursday evening Mary sensed trouble immediately.

'Where have you been today, Mary?' said Mrs Palmer.

'I've been to work.'

'You've been to work, all week? You're a *liar*. I phoned them.. You left weeks ago, they said.' Mrs Palmer's voice sounded low and it frightened Mary. It sounded menacing.

'Oh, no, not the old job, I've got a new job.' said Mary.

'Where did you get all that money?' said Mrs Palmer.

Mary looked at Rose, and avoided Dave's eye. 'What money?' she asked carefully.

'The money you had on Saturday. A lot of money. Where did you get it? What sort of job pays that kind of money? Who gave it to you?'

Then Mary saw Dave smirking and she knew. Mrs Palmer knew about the Pill. Mary was shaking, her mother knew she was on the Pill. Maybe she had found her pills; maybe she had been in her room. Then it dawned.

'It was in my bag. You took it.' Mary looked at her mother in disbelief. 'You took the money, Mum,' she said, in a frightened whisper.

'Well you got some more from somewhere,' said Mrs Palmer. 'Where did you get all that money?'

Mary looked at the three of them. Their faces seemed to her to be contorted with anger, bitterness and malice. She suddenly felt afraid in her own home. She turned and ran.

There was nowhere to go but to Mr Hartley. She knocked on his door, praying he would not be out. There was no reply. After some minutes Mary gave up telling herself that Mr Hartley was at home. She sat on his doorstep to wait. She heard the clock in the hallway in his flat strike nine, then the quarter hours until it struck ten, and then the quarter hours until it struck eleven. She was in despair. Suppose he had gone away? Several people had passed her as she sat on his step and averted their eyes. No one had spoken to her and she thought she must look a sight.

At last she heard Mr Hartley's voice. He was coming up the stairs. He was talking to someone and laughing. At first she could not place the sound. She realised she had never heard him laugh. In fact she had rarely seen him smile. He looked kindly or amiable but he rarely smiled. She stood up and tried to tidy her hair, tried to smile. As he appeared she saw that the American, Anton was with him. They did not look pleased to see her.

Coming forward unsmilingly, Mr Hartley said: 'Hello Mary, is everything all right?'

Mary was suddenly at a loss. She couldn't tell him what had

27

happened. She was acutely aware that he was hiding his displeasure. What have I done? He doesn't like me after all, she thought. What am I going to do? I can't go home.

'Come inside, Mary, you look as if you could do with a drink.'

She sat awkwardly in the living room with Anton and Mr Hartley, who had opened a bottle of champagne. He became friendlier towards her, though Anton sat without saying a word, silently drinking rather a lot of champagne. Mary wondered if he disliked her.

'Why not stay here?' said Mr Hartley when Mary finally was able to tell him about the scene at home. 'Have another drink and I'll show you your room.'

Feeling heady after three glasses of champagne, Mary followed Mr Hartley into a bedroom. She had never seen such a room. The huge brass bed was covered in black and silver-coloured silky sheets and what looked like an old-fashioned eiderdown. There were mirrors along two of the walls, and more on the celling. The lighting was strange to her; there seemed to be no light fittings, just pools of light over the bed and the wall mirrors.

Mr Hartley turned Mary with her back to him and pushed her on her knees down onto the bed. Before she could overcome her shock and with her head still spinning from the drink she'd had, Mary felt him reach round and unzip her jeans, which he pulled off, taking her knickers with them. Her face in the eiderdown, she tried to gather her thoughts. What was Mr Hartley doing? When at last she turned her head she saw he had unzipped his flies and she could see his penis. He explored her body until his fingers slipped inside her and then he slid his penis in. It felt nothing like the urgency of Stu. Mr Hartley seemed more tentative. She looked round at him again and could hardly suppress rising hysteria. He stood, erect and fully clothed, and with his eyes tight shut, thrusting blindly into her, his mouth a grim, hard line.

What is he doing this for? thought Mary. It didn't seem like the kindly Mr Hartley she thought she knew. Is it the drink? She was not enjoying it at all, and yet in a strange way she found it funny. She turned her head sideways and, in the mirror on the wall she saw her own bottom, grasped in Mr Hartley's chubby hands, going up and down, up and down. Mary began to laugh hysterically, her face buried in the eiderdown.

Suddenly it was over and Mr Hartley was saying, 'You're a good girl, Mary. You'll be all right.' And he left the room, closing the door firmly behind him.

Mary did not move until she heard music coming from somewhere in the flat. She crept to the door and opened it. She could see a light under a door along the hallway and the classical music was quite loud. She wondered if Mr Hartley had gone to sleep with the music on. There was just one room in the flat with the door closed. Mary found the bathroom and had a shower. Well, thank God; Anton must have gone home, she thought.

She lay on the black and silver bedding, looking at herself in the strangely-lit mirrors on the ceiling. She did not know what to make of Mr Hartley's behaviour. Had he fallen in love with her? Was it just the drink? She pulled back the bed-clothes and looked at herself lying on the black and silver sheets. She began to gently stroke her body and felt comforted. She lay soothing herself and looking at her reflection, remembering Mick and Stu and how soothing it had felt. It had hurt the first time, but they had soothed her with their tongues. She laughed, watching herself masturbate in the mirrored ceiling. If her mum could see her now. Her mum with her accusation: – 'What sort of job pays money like that?' And then the truth dawned.

'I'm on the game,' she said aloud. 'Only you could be on the game for several weeks without knowing it, you silly cow,' she said to her reflection.

The pattern of Mary's life was soon set. She slept late and then made her own breakfast. She was always alone at breakfast time. A cleaner came four days a week, a kindly middle-aged woman who greeted her rather stiffly. Mary, feeling profoundly embarrassed, tried to keep out of her way as much as possible.

Mr Hartley's visitors were usually in their forties and fifties, and several were from America. If there were three or four of them Mary was required to serve tea in the afternoon during their meetings. Mr Hartley wanted her to wear only a very small lace apron. She was supposed to bend from the waist to serve the tea, and she got used to the procedure which followed. It usually began with a hand stroking her behind, and then moving forward between the legs. Sometimes this led to having sex with one or another of the men there and then, though usually she left for the bedroom with one of the visitors, or each of them in turn.

She remembered ironically her first week with Mr Hartley; the succession of visitors just drinking tea and making polite conversation. They were deciding if they wanted to have sex with me or not, she thought grimly. And Mr Hartley was deciding whether to give me the job or not.

Anton was a regular visitor and by far the youngest man she met in Mr Hartley's flat. He was always polite to Mary, though she found him distant. She was glad he never approached her or even touched her.

Most often Mary had to sleep with just one of Mr Hartley's clients. When she got over the embarrassment it was not so difficult to do. They didn't usually want much conversation with her.

She heard the doorbell ringing while she was in the shower and ignored it. She would never open the front door when she was in the flat alone. Thinking the caller must have left she walked into the hall. The letterbox flipped open and she saw a pair of large, heavily made-up blue eyes staring at her.

'Come on, Mary, let me in. Hartley told me to come. I'm Suzy.' She was a girl of about Mary's own age, who walked past Mary in a cloud of cigarette smoke. 'I've come to ginger you up a bit.'

'Ginger me up?'

Suzy patted Mary's crotch. 'Yeah, ginger you up. These old boys like a bit of lezzie sex. I'm here to show yer'.

30

'I don't. I can't,' said Mary.

'Come on, it only seems strange for the first ten minutes,' said Suzy. She looked hard at Mary and then said, 'Let's have a drink. We can do it a bit pissed tonight, if you like. They won't mind.'

Suzy found some champagne and expertly popped the cork, swigging it straight from the bottle so that the white bubbles trickled down her chin. Laughing, she took off her dress and began anointing her body with the bubbles.

'Do what?' asked Mary.

'Some sad old bastards want a lezzie floor show,' replied Suzy. 'Come on, it'll be all right. Just think about what you like and do it to me. Look, I'll show you.' Suzy took off her G-string. She had small, round breasts with hard, dark little nipples. Her body had an attractive smattering of freckles and her pubic hair was a bright carroty red, in contrast to the hair on her head, which was bleached very blonde and cut short. 'Come on Mary, come on, I've got a living to make.'

They lay on the bed and Suzy took Mary's breasts gently in her hands, caressing them and licking the nipples, softly at first, then harder. 'OK, that wasn't so bad, was it? Now you do it to me. Come on, don't look so gobsmacked!'

Mary did not move.

'Okay, next demo,' said Suzy. 'I'm just going to stroke your cunt and slide my fingers in. Then I'll fuck you with my tongue. Honest, that's all we have to do. The old boys like that. I do it to you, you do it to me, we do it to each other, you know, like proper oral sex.'

She began gently stroking Mary, running her fingers up and down the lips, parting them gently. Then she ran her tongue slowly over Mary's clitoris, gradually speeding up the movement. She stopped. 'Oh come on Mary, I'm not sticking pins in you. We have to put on a *show*. That's what Hartley's old boys want. It won't hurt, and they pay me good money. It's all right for you Mary, you've got Hartley. You don't have to find money for fags and rent. You don't have a useless git of a boyfriend to support. So stop pissing about and come on.'

31

Mary closed her eyes as Suzy began again, kissing and caressing her nipples, running her hands all over her body and licking her, making loud, slurping noises. 'Oh, smile for Chrissakes, Mary,' she said. 'I didn't think I was that useless. Come on, Mary, just shut your eyes and stick out your tongue, I'll do the rest.'

It was a strange sensation. Suzy rubbed herself against Mary's tongue, moaning and sighing, taking Mary's hands and clasping them to her small, hard breasts. The pubic hair in her mouth shocked Mary and she pulled back, opening her eyes in horror.

'Jeesus, Mary, you're a hopeless shag. You'd better shift yourself tonight,' said Suzy. 'How come you let all those blokes bugger you, wank all over you and sit on your face till you choke, but you won't do something with me that won't hurt and you might even like, if you let yourself.'

'Because it's not right,' said Mary.

'So, some tired old sod who keeps his pyjamas on at home coming all over your face is right, then?' said Suzy contemptuously. 'You can't tell me that if I lick you till you come it won't be fun, because I won't believe you. I promise I won't use my teeth.'

Mary took a swig of champagne. 'Go easy on that, Mary,' said Suzy. 'We don't want to be incapable tonight. You can save the drink for later, we won't just get away with fucking each other, mate.'

Mary was swigging champagne. 'There's one,' she said, 'he must be sixty, if he's a day. And he grinds away, and every time he says the same thing: "Am I right up you, am I right up you?" like he thinks his dick is so huge it reaches my neck. And I want to say to him, "Right up where? What are you on about?" One day I just put my hand over his mouth, and do you know, he looked at me in surprise, he looked at me as if he'd never seen me before, or forgotten I was there. He might just as well have been at home wanking. The silly wanker.'

She and Suzy collapsed, laughing, and finished the champagne.

3

There was someone at the door. No one was expected. It was a Sunday and Rose's twelfth birthday but no party had been planned for her. The family expected no one to call. Mum and dad had bought her a wristwatch, her first one, and Rose was very proud of it. She was planning to wear it to school the next day and her mother was warning her against it, telling her she was bound to lose it. The doorbell rang again.

John Palmer had gone out to his allotment early that morning, his usual practice on Sundays. Mary saw her mother open the front door to a policeman and heard him say: 'I'm afraid your husband has passed away.' Suddenly stopping as if lost for words, perhaps thinking he had spoken too soon, the policeman looked past Mrs Palmer and saw Rose and Mary. It seemed to make him feel uncomfortable.

'Perhaps the children . . .?' he said. Mrs Palmer turned slowly towards Mary and Rose, who hovered uncertainly in the hallway behind her. Mary was frightened by the look on her mother's face; desperation mixed with anger. Mary could recall that moment clearly, the moment she heard, without fully taking it in, that her father was dead.

She stood with Rose in the tiny back yard. She thought she recalled the policeman suggesting the children should play in the garden. Had he really suggested that? Did he expect them to go out and play when their father had just died? It wasn't until much later that it occurred to her that he would not have taken them for the children of the deceased. The dead man was 68 years old. They'd be his grandchildren, perhaps, but not his children. That is if the policeman had given their relationship any thought at all. Mary sensed even then his realisation that he had spoken too quickly. He had blurted out his news at the front door, instead of coming into the house, giving Mrs Palmer the opportunity to sit down, even acknowledging the two little girls, instead of sending them into the back yard with those terrible words in their ears: 'I'm afraid your husband has passed away.'

Mary clutched Rose's arm. 'Passed away means dead, doesn't it?' she said.

'No, no,' said Rose. 'It doesn't. It *can't*.'

A trickle of relatives came awkwardly into the room where Molly Palmer sat crying quietly, wordlessly acknowledging their 'sorrys', not hearing their apologies. It was as if shame had come upon the family.

Mr Palmer's daughter by his first marriage, Joyce, a sullen, uncommunicative woman, told Mrs Palmer: 'You have nothing to reproach yourself for. You made him very happy.' She left shortly afterwards.

Or had Mary imagined those words, too? Why should Mrs Palmer have had anything to reproach herself for in marrying Joyce's widowed father? Because she had married him at a time in his life when he might have been better left to his allotment and the pub? For burdening him with two children when most men of his age were grandfathers, which, indeed he was already to Joyce's children, and to those of his sons John and Harry? Why should her mother reproach herself? Had she hurt Joyce by marrying her father? It was not until years later, after the family on Mary's father's side had drifted away, leaving Mrs Palmer's brother Pete their only relative that Mary realised she had somehow taken on that reproach for herself. Had by association accepted responsibility for her father's death, for making him take on the burden of another family so late in his life. A burden which had killed him.

John Palmer was a quiet man who liked his pipe and his allotment, an uncommunicative man who was loving to his children in a detached way, who often seemed preoccupied. It was not until she had grown up that Mary realised she had always blamed herself for her father's death. He had left them. Left the unspoken tension which hung in the house

34

like the smoke from his pipe, left the wife and children he could not communicate with, to die peacefully from a sudden coronary in the place he was happiest: his beloved allotment.

A few days after the policeman came, on the way to school, Mary met a girl from her class with her older sister. 'We saw the copper at your house,' said the older girl. 'My dad said your dad is dead.'

'Yes,' said Mary, hanging her head. Her classmate, with a sudden rush of sympathy, said she was sorry. Mary looked at them both helplessly, feeling embarrassed, feeling ashamed.

The same girl had said to her just a couple of weeks before, 'Why has your dad got white hair? He looks older than my granddad.' And Mary remembered sadly that she had asked her father why he didn't dye his hair.

Mary and Rose did not go to their father's funeral. Their mother did not consult them but told an elderly neighbour that they were too young. Neither of them questioned their mother. They went instead to spend the day with the elderly neighbour.

Mrs Amis drank from bottles of Guinness, placing the empties carefully in a carrier bag to take back to the off-licence. She swore that Guinness was food. It made her strong, she said.

'I knew I'd see *him* out,' Mrs Amis chuckled. 'He's not the man he was. He was never the same after young Ruth died.'

'Who wasn't?' asked Rose.

Mrs Amis stared ahead of her, her thick matted grey hair in a tangle about her head. She swigged from her bottle, wiping her mouth noisily with the back of one grimy hand. 'Him, that John Palmer. She died in his arms, they couldn't save her. And he was never the same after that,' she said with apparent satisfaction. 'That other one, she's not a patch on 'er. Ruth was the apple of his eye, so pretty and clever, she was, he was so proud of her. No one else could touch her.' She suddenly looked straight at Rose and made as if to get up out of her chair, fumbling and finally giving up, falling backwards with her legs apart. She smelled horribly of stale pee. Rose and Mary edged towards the door.

'She's away with the fairies,' whispered Rose. 'She'll have forgot we're here.'

'Now, dear take me empties back, there's a good girl,' Mrs Amis said. 'And bring me back the money.'

'Who, Mrs Amis?' said Rose, coming forward again. 'Who died in dad's arms? Who are you talking about?'

Mary felt uneasy. She stood, unable to move, wishing she had the nerve to turn and run.

'Her mother went soon afterwards,' said Mrs Amis. 'That was a funny business as well. They're in the same grave,' she added with a noisy smack of her wet lips. 'And now he's gone and married again, and them not gone a year. No. He's not the same man at all.' She sat swigging her Guinness, rocking backwards and forwards in her chair.

'Come on, Mare,' whispered Rose. 'She's forgotten we're here. I'm not taking any empties back. She's crazy. Come on; let's go home. How come she stinks so much, and doesn't know?'

'It's the drink,' said Mary.

The days and weeks after her father's death merged together. Mary felt numb. She could barely recall going to school and yet she supposed she must have done. Her mother returned to work. Long silences became routine at the Palmer household. Christmas came and went, their first Christmas without their dad. All three of them got flu and spent the new year in bed.

It was three years before Mary went to see her father's grave. She stood staring at the headstone:

Treasured memories of a much loved husband and father,
John Palmer, who passed away 3rd October 1958, aged 68

Mary looked around the graveyard, childishly hoping for some kind of sign that her father hadn't entirely gone away. She wished she believed in ghosts. She walked back towards the entrance, reluctantly thinking she should go home. She

36

began idly reading the gravestones. She noticed that another gravestone bore the name 'Palmer'. And then she stopped suddenly, shocked by what she had just read:

In loving memory of our precious Ruth, taken so suddenly from us aged 19 years. And of Nancy Palmer, mother of Ruth and dear wife of John.

Mary read and re-read the stone in disbelief. It must be a mistake. It must be some other Palmers. She remembered her half-sister Joyce's daughter Sylvia saying when they were children together that one of the biggest sadnesses in her life was that she had not known her Granny Nancy.

She remembered Mrs Amis saying, 'She died in his arms. They couldn't save her.' And then she remembered, 'They're in the same grave.' She had to ask someone about this. Who could she ask? She watched her mother very closely that evening. Could she ask her? Would she be angry? Would it upset her? Maybe her mother didn't know about Ruth. No, she couldn't ask her. She couldn't ask Mrs Amis, she had died. There was no one she could ask about Ruth.

Unless she asked Joyce? She rarely saw her half-sister and brothers. Could she go and ask them? She worried at it. In the end she decided not to. They would not want to see her. How they must have hated their dad remarrying so soon after they'd lost first their sister and then their mum. How they must have hated me and Rose, she thought. How sad Dad must have been to have lost a daughter so young. So sad he could not speak about her or have any photographs of her. Had she been ill? Why did she die? Had it been a horrible disease? So unspeakable that it had to be kept from her and Rose? Mary fretted about the disease. Could it be hereditary? Would she die at 19 as well?

Ruth must have died at home if she had died in her dad's arms, she thought. Maybe she was killed in a road accident. Maybe it had happened outside the house and then she had died in her dad's arms. How could she find out? There was no one to ask. How sad her dad must have been. No wonder he was so quiet. If only I had known, I would have been nicer to him, thought Mary. I would never have asked him why he didn't dye his hair if I had known.

4

Mary was not sure when she first became aware that Mr Hartley and Anton were lovers. She was used to them being often together and gradually realised that when Anton stayed the night it was in Mr Hartley's room. She remembered her first night and the music coming from Mr Hartley's room – she had assumed then that Anton had left, but of course he had been with Mr Hartley and the music had been deliberately loud so that Mary would not hear them.

Mary felt shy of Mr Hartley. She could never call him Geoffrey and continued to call him Mr Hartley. She noticed that Anton called him Hartley, but this seemed to be as a term of affection. Gradually she realised that everyone called him Hartley and began to do the same.

Mary felt more comfortable with Anton who, she decided, was not cold and standoffish after all. He simply did not know what to say to girls. She had never met a homosexual before; such things had never been mentioned at home. She laughed now to think that no sex of *any* kind had ever been mentioned at home. Marty's conception was assumed by Mrs Palmer to have been the result of Dave having got Rose drunk. Mary had accepted this as the truth and had been shocked when Rose had later told her that she and Dave had been having sex regularly since they'd met – she was just unlucky on one occasion.

It seemed bizarre to Mary that she was fond of Hartley. How could she be fond of someone who had done what he had done to her? The fact that her seduction had been as hysterically funny as it had been shocking had somehow overshadowed the indignity. Mary laughed about it to herself.

No wonder he had stood there erect with his eyes closed and his tie in place; he had fucked her out of professional duty. He had simply performed an initiation he must have seen as routine. He had been as glad when it was over as Mary herself had been, knowing that she was fuckable, and therefore employable, but that he would not have to do it again.

At the beginning of November Hartley announced that Anton had to return to the States to work and that Hartley and Mary were to go as well.

'But how can I go?' said Mary. 'I've never been abroad. I haven't got a passport or anything.' Mary felt a strange, panicky feeling. She did not want to leave London. She felt afraid. Hartley told her it would be easy to get a passport and she could get a visitor's visa as she had somewhere to stay.

'Is it a holiday, then?' asked Mary, knowing that it wasn't, feeling that she had no choice but to do whatever Hartley wanted her to do.

'Well, yes, in a way. We're going to California so you'll be able to see the sights. It'll be very exciting for you. Anton's father is in the film industry and he has lots of connections.'

Mary stayed silent. So now they weren't clients, they were 'connections'. 'That's an interesting word for it,' she said, suddenly shocked at her own cynicism.

'Don't worry Mary,' said Hartley kindly. 'We'll look after you, you know that.' He took out his wallet and handed Mary £250. 'Go and get yourself some new clothes,' he said.

They were to be in California until the new year. Mary felt confused. What could she do? She did not want to go home, that was certain. Hartley had been kind to her and now she was fond of him. The alternative to going to America was unthinkable. Mary knew that she would find it very hard to find a job. And she could not go back home.

Suddenly Hartley's father died and they had to delay their trip so that he could go to the funeral. He and Anton talked for hours about Hartley's loss and Mary felt no part of it. She was unable to ask Hartley how it felt, and she had uncomfortable feelings about the loss of her own father which had again

40

resurfaced. She was beginning to think she should not go to the States. She should go and see her mother.

She had tried to put her family out of her mind, but the death of Hartley's father made her think of them again, and with the memory of them came thoughts about Ruth. She felt again the need to speak to someone about her, someone who had known what she was like before she got ill. She waited until Hartley was alone and then tried to broach the subject with him. He was drinking whisky and poured a glass for Mary, which she downed without thinking.

He talked bitterly about his father, a retired doctor. Hartley had a younger brother whom his dad had always favoured. Christopher wanted to follow his father into medicine from an early age, 'just to show me up,' said Hartley. 'I was a dunce at science. And Christopher certainly wasn't out to help humanity. He doesn't actually like people. He's now a Harley Street specialist and very rich indeed.'

'You didn't get on with your dad?' asked Mary tentatively, wishing not for the first time that she didn't have the knack of saying the wrong thing in sensitive situations.

'No, I hated him,' said Hartley vehemently. 'I could never do anything right in his eyes. I was no good at science or games. There was obviously no point in my trying to get into university. He told me so. Christopher was always the favoured one.' He poured another glass of whisky and downed it. 'The worst bloody thing about going to this bloody funeral,' he said, 'will be bloody Christopher and his God-awful, tarty, rich bitch of a wife.'

'But you're rich Hartley,' said Mary.

Hartley snorted. 'I'm not rich, I wheel and deal. I'm not a *professional*.' He gave the word an elongated sarcasm. 'I'm the waster of the family, they don't invite me to any of their shindigs, except this one of course. But how *respectable* he is, this Harley Street ponce. He's no better than me. He doesn't think taking rich bastards' money to rearrange their sad bodies is poncing. We're in the same game, St Christopher and I.'

'What about your mum?' asked Mary. 'Does she, er, know

41

what you do?' Her voice trailed off. She had forgotten, briefly, what Hartley was to her. She found herself pouring another drink to give herself something to do. She suddenly felt too shy to pour one for Hartley. It confused her that she needed Hartley so much, even trusted and relied on him. It didn't make sense. He was her pimp. He made her feel wanted and trashy at the same time. He was the only family she had now.

'Oh, she'll be nagging at me, they've always thought of me as a waster. What Ma knows precisely, I don't know. If she does know, she never says.'

Mary was not sure if he meant the pimping or the homosexuality. Maybe his mother knew about both.

'But she is very worldly, you know,' he went on. 'She was very seductive in her day. The old man couldn't keep up with her, and she always had lovers.' He laughed suddenly. 'Still has lovers, some of them half her age. If she does know, she doesn't say. . .' He stopped suddenly and his eyes filled with tears. He sat staring at his whisky glass, letting the tears fall. Then he got up slowly and heavily. 'But still that shouldn't stop me from inheriting now that the old bugger has finally died.'

'I had a sister who died,' said Mary.

'What? What's her name? Rose? She isn't dead, is she?'

'No, another one, a half-sister, I don't know why she died, but she was only nineteen. She died in my father's arms.'

Hartley snorted. 'Died in your father's arms? That's a bit Barbara Cartland,' he said, then stopped laughing when he saw that Mary was really upset.

'I don't know how she died,' she snivelled.

'When was this?' asked Hartley.

'Don't know, sometime before my Dad married my Mum. His wife died as well.'

'Sounds very odd, Mary, his wife and his daughter die, then he marries again.'

'What are you saying, what do you mean?' Mary suddenly felt uneasy.

Seeing her ashen face, Hartley said hurriedly, 'Well, it

shouldn't be hard to find out. You just go to Somerset House and look at the death certificates. Do you know her name?'

'She was called Ruth Palmer and I suppose I could work out when it was. I don't know when exactly, though.'

'Well, you just look up all the Ruth Palmers. There shouldn't be that many to choose from. You can do that while I'm at the funeral. We can't delay our trip for much longer.'

Ruth Anne Palmer, aged 19 years. Died by her own hand from an overdose of aspirin whilst the balance of her mind was disturbed.

Mary wished she had not come. What good had it done her to know that her half-sister had killed herself? She read the entry again. 'Whilst the balance of her mind was disturbed'. What had happened to her? Why had she killed herself at 19? What is the point, thought Mary. I will never know.

5

Mary was excited about going on a plane for the first time. Hartley let her have the seat by the window. She had an unexpected feeling of elation as she sat looking at the distant airport buildings. She would be glad to leave London behind after all. There didn't seem to be anything for her there now.

Mary was left to herself in the apartment for the first day after their arrival in Los Angeles. It was a lovely apartment. Best of all she liked the view across the rooftops to the bay. Mary spent the whole day looking out of the window.

She needed more clothes for the work in LA. There were more parties to attend and people to meet. Too shy to say much, Mary contented herself with observing people. If a client liked her then she would stay with him for the evening, returning later to his hotel room.

She realised she had never really pieced together Hartley's 'connections'. Of course, even in London they had been directly or indirectly attached to the film industry. That must have been how Hartley met Anton's father, she thought. I wonder what Anton Sr. made of his son falling in love with silly old Hartley, she thought. It made the whole situation very funny when she considered how highly regarded the old man was in film circles.

One evening Mary was alone in the apartment. Hartley and Anton had gone to have drinks with some British people, who apparently had no need of Mary's services. It was good to have the apartment to herself. She stood by the window, gazing out at the bay. She was startled to hear the apartment door open behind her and turned to see Simon.

'Mary, how nice to see you again,' he said, laughing. 'Well, say something, Mary, or I'll think you're not pleased to see me.'

At first Mary could not speak. Finally she said lamely, 'What are you doing here?'

'I work in Hollywood now,' said Simon. I'm working on a couple of films. They need some expert British input.' He laughed his old confident laugh.

'But how did you. . .' Mary's voice trailed off and she stood in stunned silence. She looked at Simon's face and she knew with absolute certainty. 'It was you, wasn't it? You knew Hartley didn't you? He didn't pick me up by accident?'

Simon placed his hand on his chest and bowed in mock apology. '*Mea culpa, mea culpa*,' he said, laughing loudly.

'But why did you do it?'

'I couldn't let you go on the way you were. That dragon of a mother of yours. No sixteen-year-old should live alone with such an embittered old bag, let alone a girl like you. You took yourself so seriously, Mary. No one was allowed to laugh in your presence without you thinking they were laughing at you. So we laughed at you all the more.' He saw Mary's hurt face. 'Oh not everyone, you silly girl. Rollo and I, I mean. Some people just laugh, Mary, because life amuses them. You were totally obsessed by what your mother would think. You were old before your time.'

'And what am I now?' said Mary bitterly. 'Mum wasn't like, like you say. Simon, she had such a sad life.'

'So you thought the best you could do for her was to be the same.' He came towards her. 'I decided to rescue you. Oh not immediately, and it wasn't planned quite as much as you might think. But I knew if I left it to you, you'd end up like your mother, or marry some clod, like your sister did. I showed you a way out, you silly girl. I decided you ought to be something else. There are enough poisonous old bags like your mother already.' He gently touched her face, and said almost tenderly, 'You were so . . . perfect. Lovely little face

45

and a wonderful body, and that wild, disobedient hair. And that look you used to get. The look of a frightened rabbit, poised just before it ran away. Rollo and I used to laugh at you, but we both thought you were sweet.'

'But you didn't want me . . . that time . . .' The words were choking Mary, but she continued. 'That time in your flat, you didn't want me. You made sure that I wanted you and then you turned your back on me.'

'You're reading too much into that, Mary, believe me,' said Simon. 'It wasn't that.' He stopped, as if he couldn't remember.

It ruined my life, and this bastard can't even remember, thought Mary.

'Anyway I did you a favour, believe me, Mary. I didn't just want to keep you for myself. I wasn't trying to make you into something sad or do anything to hurt you. You just needed waking up. I didn't do anything to you, as I recall. It suddenly seemed too messy.' He laughed. He had an arrogant way of making obscure jokes and then laughing at his own assumed cleverness.

'You can't even remember,' said Mary.

'I just thought it better not to,' he went on as if she had not spoken. 'You'd only have got pregnant, or something silly like that. And you were the sort of over-dependent type who would think you were in love with me. You'd think if I fucked you it meant I was going to marry you.'

'But how could you just find me a pimp like that, Simon, without telling me?'

'You would have run away if I'd told you. And anyway, you were asking me. You were begging me. You wanted me to save you; you were desperate for salvation, Mary. When you left the agency you didn't stay at home like a good girl, you kept coming back, hanging round the scene of the crime. There you were, every day, haunting the West End. It was then I told Hartley about you. Better he pick you up than a real bastard.'

'What do you mean?'

'Someone would have picked you up eventually.'

46

'No, no, they wouldn't. Why would they?' said Mary helplessly.

'From the Virgin Mary to Mary Magdalen in, how long has it been – a couple of months?' he said. 'And I hear you're good.'

'It wasn't inevitable at all,' said Mary. 'It wasn't like that.' Simon looked at her with mock gravity. 'But I could have been . . .'

'Beaten, raped or tortured? Humiliated, injected with drugs by God knows who? No, Mary, I knew Hartley and his boys. The worst you might have got was the pox. I told him. I knew you wouldn't have to service any psychos.'

'You didn't know that, you didn't!' said Mary in a small, shaky voice. 'Unless you knew all along what was going on. Of course you've been in touch with Hartley all along. It was your idea we came here. Nothing to do with Anton at all.'

Simon continued as if she had not spoken. 'Just a bit of suburban fucking.'

Mary remembered the routine in London, the procession of men who thought anal or oral sex was the extreme of naughtiness, who'd probably never been asked or thought of asking anyone what they wanted. 'But you didn't know, Simon, no one can be sure what people might do.' Then she remembered Stu and Mick and what a laugh it had been. Stu's joke about decorating the ceiling made her laugh again. 'I'm only going to do it for fun from now on, Simon,' she said.

'Well, now you've got your sense of humour in place, how about starting with me?'

'No, I couldn't, Simon, not with you.'

He laughed at her. 'You will, you'll change your mind before you go back to London. Hartley hasn't got anything better on offer for you.'

'No, Simon, I won't change my mind,' said Mary. 'And what's more, I'm going back to London now.'

Simon looked at her gravely. 'You've changed Mary. And good for you. Go back to London, then, if Hartley will let you. He's very pleased with your work, you know. He'll take some persuading.'

'Don't pretend you care, Simon,' said Mary. 'You *don't* care, you never have cared what happens to me, and now you have the nerve to laugh at me after what you've done,' said Mary. 'Yes I did think I was in love with you. I went on the Pill for you. I thought that was what you wanted me to do. When you rejected me I didn't care what happened to me any more.'

'Well, more fool you, baby,' said Simon. 'You should have had more self-respect. If you're not careful you'll out-martyr your appalling mother.'

6

The next evening there was a party in Malibu. Mary decided it was to be her last. She was to speak to Hartley. She was going to persuade him to let her go home.

Mary hardly recognised the person she saw reflected in the mirror. She had been sent to the beauty parlour and her hair and face were someone else's idea of gaudy chic. She was wearing the dress Hartley had bought her for her birthday. It was cut too low and Mary hated it. Of course I don't recognise myself, she told her reflection. I look like a tart. And I don't want that. I don't want to be a tart. She was suddenly horrified at herself. Simon was right. She had no self-respect. Everyone who met her knew she was a prostitute. How could she just accept that? She hated Simon now. She was going to have to face him one more time and then she was determined to return to London. She wished she did not have to go to this last party, but Hartley was counting on her.

She saw Simon across the room, and with him was Mireille. When Simon saw Mary he came over, smiling. 'Hi there, Mary, let me introduce you to my wife.' Mireille smiled a perfect smile, showing perfect white teeth. Her hair was smooth and glossy and she was wearing an expensive evening dress, simply cut, to devastating effect.

Mary could not avoid the comparison between them: the cool, beautiful, respectable young woman in a discreetly alluring dress and the little painted tart, wearing a dress that pinched in her waist and emphasised her nearly-naked breasts. My dress puts me on show, for whoever might want me, she thought. Hers just quietly says that she is desirable but unattainable. She is married to Simon.

49

Mary could see that everyone looking was looking at Mireille, who smiled at Mary and held out her hand, saying in prettily accented English: 'It is very nice to meet someone from London. Simon and I met there, and I love it.'

Mary knew that Mireille had not recognised her. She managed to say hello and then, as politely as she could, to take her leave. She watched Mireille from the other side of the room for the rest of the evening. She had a slow, sweet smile. She appeared to speak very little and yet she was able to draw people to her. And yet she is safe, thought Mary, bitterly. Safe because she is married to Simon. Feeling her humiliation complete, Mary went to find Hartley.

'I have to speak to you, now,' she said.

'Not now, later, please Mary,' said Hartley.

'*Now*, Hartley,' said Mary with such severity that Hartley looked sharply at her and then relented. They walked out onto the terrace. 'Hartley I'm getting out. I can't do this any more.'

'It's a hard world out there, Mary. You'd be eaten alive.'

'There's something I hardly know how to say, Hartley. You've been so kind to me and the clients have – been OK – some sad old sods but no one has really hurt me. Look, can we go somewhere?'

Hartley ushered her out into the street where he called a taxi to take them back to their apartment.

'I've started to get uncomfortable feelings about my Dad. He was old, my Dad. He'd retired by the time I was four. I spent a lot of time with him, I was the youngest and he was a bit distant, but gentle. He didn't always have a lot to say, but he used to make me laugh. I used to sit on his lap, and the smell of him . . . it's mixed up in my mind now . . . it was the smell of his shirt. Always so fresh and clean, a dried-on-the-washing-line-clean. And his face was so pink, and he must have shaved often because he was so soft. And sometimes with your old men, they . . . it isn't right, Hartley, all these old men. After what Simon said, he seemed to blame my Mum for everything. But I think it was my Dad dying like that,

50

leaving me like that, that made me what I am. I can't do it any more, Hartley.

She was sobbing now and Hartley made to put his arms around her, then withdrew.

'I never said goodbye to him. I wasn't asked to his funeral. He just went away.' She was shaking now and crying uncontrollably.

'It's all right Mary, don't cry,' said Hartley, dabbing in an ineffectual way at her face with a tissue, not knowing what else to do. 'You go home, Mary, back to London. I can find another . . .' He stopped, embarrassed. He had been going to say 'another tart'. 'You go back to London. You can stay in the flat until you find something. I won't bother you. You phone me here if you need anything.' He moved away from her, unable to say any more. Mary had forgotten he was there. She stood staring out of the window. She could see the lights and the beautiful bay and the outline of the rooftops. She could marvel at how still and calm and perfect they all were with a sense entirely separate from the choking grief she was feeling.

'I'll book you a flight tonight. You can have the flat, Mary. Don't worry about anything, baby.' Mary did not hear him. He went back to his room and booked her on the first available flight to London.

51

7

It felt strange returning to the Mount Street flat alone. It was very clean and tidy; Mary supposed the cleaner must still come on her usual days. Hartley must be putting money into her account too, thought Mary. She did not want to bump into her. She could no longer maintain any innocence about what she had been doing there. I've been like a sleepwalker, or a wind-up toy she thought, just doing what other people told me to do. She remembered Mick and Stu, who seemed to be the only real people she had ever met. Why can't I just be myself like they are?

She did not want to sleep in her old bedroom with its mirrors and its memories. She moved into a small boxroom, which had just a bed and wardrobe with hardly any room to move about. With all the doors locked she felt safe.

She spent her days window-shopping. She was amazed at the Christmas lights in Oxford Street and Regent Street; she had never seen their like. She had been to Oxford Street only once with her mother, to the sales. They had come back with nothing and her mother had declared 'never again, there was nothing worth looking at.'

Mrs Palmer's life, never very full, had narrowed after the death of her husband. Money was very tight and she hated Christmas. Mary had often wondered why this was. Had her mother always hated it? Or was it because she could not afford to buy herself or her children much? She did her best for her daughters with little money but it was always a lonely time.

Mr Palmer was a quiet man, but Mary had occasionally glimpsed a sense of humour. Had he suppressed this since his marriage to a woman for whom everything seemed to be a joyless duty? What did he see in her mum? Mary recalled with a sense of shame that her mother had once said that her husband did not want to be lodger in his own house after his first wife had died.

Joyce and her husband had been living with him. Mary felt the familiar feeling of guilt and shame. Had her dad married her mum just so he would not become poor old dad confined to the back room? Why does no one say what they mean. . .?

As usually happened when she thought of her dad Mary began to think of Ruth. Why did Dad never talk about her? He was my dad but he never told me I'd had another sister. Was he ashamed that he could do nothing to prevent her suicide? Why had Ruth killed herself at nineteen? Mary suddenly found that she was crying.

She stopped at a shop to dry her eyes and saw a card in the window. A local florist shop was looking for a junior to learn the trade. She went in, intending to say that she had left school in July and gone to stay with a family in California. She knew she could rely on Hartley to back her up. But the manageress did not ask for a reference. She seemed to like Mary and said she could start on Saturday, on a week's trial.

Mary enjoyed the work, learning to make bouquets and to tie bows. It felt peaceful to be among flowers and she enjoyed talking to the customers. The women in the shop were friendly enough, but Mary did not talk much about herself to them.

She spent her evenings alone in Hartley's flat, drinking. It became a compulsion. She watched television and she drank and she forgot about herself. She did not want to go out. She did not want to encounter any of the other people in the building. She began to have hangovers and to sleep late. She could not afford to lose her job. It wasn't the money – Hartley had put £1,000 into her bank account from the States – she just didn't want to spend all her days as well as her evenings alone in the flat.

She was trying not to think that Christmas was only four days away. The women in the shop all had plans and asked

53

Mary what she was going to do. She decided to take all the booze to her mother's house on Christmas Eve.

Leaving the matronly celebrations at the shop early, Mary went to Oxford Street and found Selfridges still open. She had some expensive chocolates gift-wrapped for her mother and sister. Then she remembered Marty. How could she have forgotten him until now? She bought him a little wooden train with an engine and three carriages, and a little cloth rabbit. It was only when she returned to the flat to collect overnight things and the booze that she asked herself: Why a rabbit? She could imagine Simon's amusement that of all the toy animals she might have chosen she had unthinkingly chosen a rabbit.

She took a taxi to Tottenham and got out some yards away from her old home. She could not bring herself to knock at the door. Several times she walked away and then back again, burdened by the alcohol and the presents. She made herself walk up to the door. She realised she had nothing for Dave. He can have the booze, she thought. She was dreading seeing him, in particular, and wondered why she had come. They would probably not be pleased to see her. She had better not stay long. She would say she had to get back to work. Maybe I'll go back anyway, she thought.

The thought of spending Christmas Day watching television and drinking alone in Hartley's flat made Mary knock at the door. Rose opened it. She was wearing an old pair of jeans and a man's shirt. She looked as if she had been crying. She did not look happy to see her sister.

Mrs Palmer was tearfully pleased to see Mary but soon the questions began. Where had she been? Why had she run off like that? Why did she never consider anyone but herself? Mrs Palmer said she had been worried sick. While Rose was out of the room she said: 'He left her, that husband of hers, as soon as he knew she was pregnant again.'

'Didn't she go on the Pill, then?' said Mary, immediately wishing she hadn't mentioned that word.

Mrs Palmer looked at her sharply but said nothing. Hur-

54

riedly changing the subject, Mary said: 'Come on Mum, let's open the presents now.'

'Where did you get the money to buy those?' asked her mother. 'And all that drink? I thought you just worked in a shop.'

'Oh, I get tips,' said Mary. 'And I clean the flat for them as well, and I get my keep because I cook and look after things . . .' Her voice trailed lamely.

Rose came back into the room and eagerly accepted a glass of wine. Mrs Palmer and Rose sat watching television without speaking. Mary wished she had stayed in the flat.

I would rather be on my own there than live here, she thought. She wished she had an excuse to go. Despite all that had happened to her, her situation was preferable to Rose's. It seems so unfair, she said to herself. What choice was there between what happened to Rose and what happened to me? Maybe Mum was right after all, that choices are only for people with money.

She was looking forward to seeing Marty with his presents on Christmas morning. It was the only thing that kept her from leaving. Rose opened the parcel with the train for him and ran it around him while he squealed with delight. He tore open the parcel with the rabbit himself and chuckled when he banged it up and down on the carpet.

'I thought you were going on the Pill,' said Mary when her mother was out of earshot.

'Dave and I weren't getting along well about the time you left,' said Rose. 'And by the time I got around to going to the doctors, I was pregnant. Dave left, like I knew he would.'

Mary did not want to ask why: she did not want to have a conversation about Dave.

The news that Uncle Pete was coming to have Christmas dinner with them made Mary stiffen with alarm. 'Oh, I can't stay to dinner, mum,' she said. 'I have to go back and cook for the family.'

'They won't expect you on Christmas Day. You have to be with your family,' said Mrs Palmer. 'And anyway, Pete will want to see you. He was very upset when you left. I'll phone and tell him you're here. He'll be so pleased.'

The hour of Uncle Pete's arrival was approaching. Mary was glad she was wearing a simple jumper and jeans and no make-up. She wanted nothing to provoke any comment from Uncle Pete. She had met his like over and over at the flat in Mount Street.

Her mother said, 'Didn't you bring a dress?'

'No, I'm all right like this Mum,' she said. 'I feel more comfortable like this.'

'You can't wear those awful jeans on Christmas Day,' said her mother. 'Rose will lend you something of hers.'

The doorbell rang and Rose went to answer it. Mary could hear Uncle Pete's voice in the hallway, loudly chivvying her sister and Rose's meek replies. He walked into the room and looked straight at Mary.

'Hello, deserter,' he said.

8

Mary spent the new year alone, having got away by promising her family they could come and see her in the shop on her first day back after the holiday.

The women in the shop cooed over Marty and chatted to Mrs Palmer and Rose. Mary could see their satisfaction that at last they could place her in some sort of background. Mary stood by awkwardly. Rose and her mum seemed so at ease with the women, more at ease than Mary was. They were all laughing. How can mum and Rose laugh like that when their lives are so awful? It didn't make sense to Mary. She thought there must be something wrong with her: that she could not feel anything or show any emotion.

She had locked all the bedroom doors at Mount Street except her own. She did not want them to see the mirrors and outrageous bedding. She felt guilty about her family. She would have liked to have given them some money. But how would she say she had come by it? She did not want any more accusations. She walked with them to the tube station and waved goodbye. They made a pathetic little group. She didn't want to see them again.

Except for Marty. She wondered if she could get Rose to let Marty stay with her for a few days. As long as she doesn't want to come as well, she thought, feeling a bitch.

As she climbed the stairs back up to Hartley's flat, she heard someone behind her and quickened her pace. She did not want to have to talk to any of the neighbours. Someone caught up with her. It was a man she vaguely recognised.

'Hello, little girl, and where have you been?' he said. He

winked and Mary was immediately on her guard. 'We were wondering what had happened to your little ménage.'

Mary felt a rising disgust and panic. The man was drunk. She could smell whisky on his breath. She fumbled for her keys. She knew she had put the Chubb lock on. It would take some time to open the door and he was right behind her. She could hear his breathing and she was afraid. As she reached the door she heard the phone ringing in the flat. The man heard it too, and hesitated. She opened the door quickly and then closed it in his face. It was Hartley on the phone.

'He knows who I am,' she wailed. 'He knows I'm here on my own.'

'He can't do anything. You've got nothing to worry about,' said Hartley. 'Just keep the door locked and bolted.'

'I don't feel safe here any more, Hartley,' said Mary. 'I don't want to stay here.'

She had a sudden realisation that everyone knew what she had been. The cleaning lady knew. How many others knew? Certainly that man in the corridor knew. Did all the people in the block know? And in the local shops. Hartley was getting impatient with her. 'Look, I'm coming back in a couple of weeks. You'll be all right Mary.

'No,' she said. 'I can't stay here.'

'Well go and stay with my old mum,' said Hartley. 'She's got that big house to herself now and she has staff. You won't have to do anything.'

'I think I've looked after enough of your old people,' said Mary.

'Old?' said Hartley. 'Not one of them was much more than fifty.'

'Yeah, and I'm seventeen,' she replied.

'Well, how about someone younger? I know, Simon and Mireille. They're doing really well out here. They've just bought a big house.'

'Simon and Mireille!' she screamed. 'Are you mad? What do you take me for? How could I work for Simon and Mireille?'

'Sorry, yes, of course, well someone younger, then. A nanny for some kids or something. Look, Mary I have to go now. Just make sure everything is all right and I'll let you know the details of my flight. Bye now, Mary.'

A nanny, thought Mary. Why not? And why not in the States? Why not New York? No one knows me there. She laughed out loud. How do you become a nanny? A card in a newsagent's window? No, that was my old profession. That's what they think of me here. Mary the tart, the prostitue, the woman of easy virtue. They should try it if they think it's easy, she thought grimly.

She thought of going to a nanny employment agency but who would employ a seventeen-year-old with no experience? She remembered those calculating agency women with their hard professional smiles. They would know what I am, she thought. No, I'm best avoiding agencies of any kind.

Perhaps she could try the newspapers. They might have nanny jobs. She went to Selfridges and looked at the rows of newspapers and magazines. There were so many of them. She asked an assistant if any magazines advertised jobs for nannies and was told: '*The Lady* is your best bet.'

Of all the nanny jobs there were only three that did not ask for qualifications. And only two that had phone numbers.

She called the first number. The voice which answered was loud and confident and American. Mrs Mercer wanted someone to help her with her children, a boy of two and a girl of four. She wanted an English nanny. Her father had been in London many times and told her that the English were quietly spoken and an English nanny would be a good influence on his grandkids whom, he thought, were becoming boisterous and noisy. 'What experience do you have, Mary? she asked. Thinking quickly Mary said she was looking after a six-month-old boy while his parents were in California. They were returning soon and would not need someone full-time. She thought wildly that she could borrow Marty to take to meet Mrs Mercer and her children. Mrs Mercer said she had three other people to see but that she would come to see Mary at the flat on Friday. That gave Mary three days.

She phoned Rose and suggested that she might have Marty to stay for a few days. Rose was reluctant: 'I'm the one who needs a break,' she said. Mary was determined that her sister should not spoil her plan.

'You can come and stay another time when the family aren't here,' she said. 'There's nowhere for you to sleep now. When they go away, then you *and* Marty can come.'

'We'll leave it till then,' said Rose.

Trying to sound casual, Mary said: 'OK, but they have some things for Marty, some clothes and toys and they're nearly new. Why don't I just take him out for the day on Friday? I've hardly seen anything of him. I'll just come and get him for the day and give you a break.'

Rose was silent. Mary was willing her to agree. She was determined to get that job with Mrs Mercer. 'Well, why can't I come, if it's just for a day?' said Rose. 'I never go anywhere.'

'Oh, well, come if you like,' said Mary, trying hard to sound as if she wasn't bothered. 'But it would be a better break for you if you came on your own another time. Then you can stay for a week, if you like. Please, Rose, I've never had much time with Marty.'

'And whose fault is that?' Rose snapped.

Mary made an effort to stay calm. 'Rose, isn't there something you'd like to do on Friday afternoon while I take Marty off your hands? I only want to spend some time with him. I won't mind babysitting for you any time you like when you've got two of them.' Mary felt no guilt at this last, cruel lie. She would have said anything to get Rose to lend her Marty. Rose remained silent. 'I'll come on Friday morning. And I bet you'll have thought of something you want to do by then,' she said. 'See you.'

Mary did not allow herself to think that Rose would change her mind. She bought things for Marty: a baby bath, nappies and talcum powder, baby food and some toys. She was even thinking that, if necessary, she would tell Rose the truth and bribe her to lend her Marty. But this she was keeping as the very last resort. She spent the whole of Thursday afternoon arranging the living room to look as if it was Marty's home.

On Friday morning she took a taxi to Tottenham, again deliberately wearing her jeans and jumper and no make-up. She was glad her mother was at work. To lie to Rose was one thing, but Mary did not think she could lie again to her mother without looking shamefaced.

She felt guilty about not loving her mother. She tried to remember how she had felt as a small child. She had loved her father, and taken it for granted that she loved her mother, too. But the evening she realised her mother had searched her handbag and taken her money had led to confused feelings. She could see why her mother would try to look out for her interests, and she felt guilty about not telling her as soon as she had lost her job at the agency. She suspected she just felt sorry for the woman. It was shocking to Mary that she could feel no love for her: that she should realise this gradually came as a shock.

Mary looked around the living room. It was cluttered and untidy. Marty was sleeping in the armchair, the one the cat used to use. The cat was nowhere to be seen.

'Where's Katie?' asked Mary.

'Oh, we had to give her away,' said Rose. 'Er, Mum was afraid she would scratch Marty.'

'But she was a gentle little thing,' said Mary. 'She would never scratch anyone. If anything she was shy of people.' She was suddenly angry that Katie was not there. 'She was *my* cat. Why didn't you tell me? I would have taken her.'

'We didn't know where you were, stupid,' said Rose. 'Much you cared about her when you left. She was old, anyway, and kept getting ill. Mum said it was the kindest thing.'

Tears came into Mary's eyes. 'Mum had her put to sleep, didn't she?'

Rose did not answer.

'Put to sleep, just because no one could be bothered to look after her,' said Mary.

'You mean *you* couldn't be bothered,' said Rose. She wrapped Marty warmly and reluctantly gave him to Mary. 'Where you taking him?' she asked.

Mary wanted to talk about her cat but she realised that if

61

she got upset Rose might not let her take Marty. 'Oh, I'm taking him back to the flat. The family wants to see him. They have some things for him their baby doesn't need any more. All good as new. I'll bring him back by five.' She left hurriedly and as soon as she got to the high street she hailed a cab to Oxford Street.

Mrs Mercer was due to arrive at 2 p.m. That gave Mary three hours. She bought Marty a harness so she could carry him in front of her, close against her. She loved the warmth of his little body and the smell of him. His eyes watched her face as she chatted to him. He seemed mesmerised by his new experience. She bought some little playsuits and booties and a hat. Within half an hour she had begun to have some sympathy for those women who stole babies because they could not have their own. She loved the feel of him against her. She did not want to give him back. She felt more contented than she had ever felt, and oddly more confident, walking around the shops with Marty strapped to her chest, feeling the warmth of him, and the smell of him: like a mixture of apples and soap.

With half an hour to go before Mrs Mercer's arrival, Mary fed Marty as much as he would eat. He was soon asleep on the new bedding she had bought for him on the living-room floor. She realised she had forgotten to buy him a cot. She hoped Mrs Mercer would not ask to see where the baby slept. She prepared an elaborate story about wanting to keep him close to her in the warm living room while she read.

The doorbell rang at five minutes to two. Mary tried to still the rising panic. She decided to take Marty to open the front door, so that Mrs Mercer would not wonder why he was not asleep in his cot.

Standing on the doormat, smiling at her, was the neighbour she had met on the stairs. He looked surprised when he saw Mary holding the baby. Mary froze. He was going to spoil everything. Mrs Mercer would see him and she would think it odd to find her talking to a man at the front door. Mary feared Mrs Mercer would be suspicious of her.

'Oh, hello, can I help you?' she said, blushing as he looked pointedly from her to the baby and back to her.

'Who's this, then?' he said, smirking.

'Er, I'm looking after him,' she said. 'You must go now, please. What do you want?'

'Well, little girl, you've been holding out on us,' he said. Mary could hear someone coming up the stairs.

'Please *go*,' she said in a panicky whisper as a tall, elegant woman appeared at the top of the stairs. The woman came forward, smiling.

'Are you Mary?' she said.

'Oh, Mrs Mercer, let me introduce you to my neighbour, er, Mr . . .'

The man beamed, took in Mrs Mercer with her cashmere coat, fur hat and gold jewellery and said: 'How do you do? I'm Tim Burton-Field. I live upstairs.'

'Hello,' she said. Then, looking at Mary, 'May I come in?'

Mary was afraid the situation must look all too obvious to Mrs Mercer. She tried to tell herself it was all right but feared her face would give her away. The man was grinning broadly, enjoying the situation and Mary's obvious confusion. 'Well, it was nice to meet you,' he said and, after a little hesitation during which Mrs Mercer regarded him steadily, he left.

Mary kept a firm hold of the still sleeping Marty, while Mrs Mercer looked around the living room. 'How long have you been here, Mary?' she asked.

Mary couldn't tell how well the interview was going. It felt soothing to hold onto the sleeping baby. Mrs Mercer had commented on what a good, contented baby he was and even gone into the kitchen herself to make coffee for them so as not to disturb him. Mary noticed her cool appraisal of the flat.

'How long have the Hartleys been away?' she asked.

'Oh, just ten days, and they'll be back for good next week,' said Mary. Oh God, why did I say that? She was panicking again. She'll want to come and meet them. I'll have to borrow Marty again, and where will I find a Mrs Hartley? Would Mrs Mercer believe Rose would marry someone like him? No, she's much too young. And she looks like me. She imagined Mrs Mercer was staring at her. There was no expression on her face.

'Do you get a lot of hassle from the neighbours?' she heard her say.

'Oh, the man at the door? No, no he's all right,' said Mary, praying that Mrs Mercer would not probe too deeply.

Mrs Mercer smiled and crossed her long beautiful legs elegantly. Looking Mary straight in the eyes she said: 'You are very young to be left alone like this with the baby. They must trust you.' She had a disconcerting habit of making comments which then hung in the air like questions or judgements, waiting coolly for Mary to answer them. Or give myself away, she thought grimly.

'Oh I thought it was you at the door, Mrs Mercer,' she said. 'I don't get many visitors.' Mary stopped suddenly, fearing that anything she might say might confirm the suspicions she dreaded Mrs Mercer was having. She tried to look calm, grateful that Marty's presence was having a soothing effect on her. She was happy just holding him and she began to relax. She looked at Mrs Mercer and decided she liked her. She looked younger than she sounded on the phone, no more than twenty-five, but so sure of herself and so glamorous. Mary thought again that her mother had been right – people with money did seem to be able to be what they wanted to be. Money seemed to give them confidence.

When she compared her own situation with Rose's, she saw that however precarious it was, hers offered more choices. She could tell lies to borrow her sister's baby and then spend a lot of money making it look as if she was a nanny. If it didn't work she could think of something else. She had lost nothing and had been able to spend time spoiling her nephew. It wasn't a matter of fairness, it was just luck.

Mrs Mercer said: 'I'd like you to come to New York with me next Friday. You will have sole charge of Martha and Dan including fixing their meals and hearing Martha read. You will have two days off every week and your keep plus pocket money. You will have your own room and TV, and your own

64

bathroom. You will have one long weekend off every six weeks. I would like you to work on a three-month trial basis. If things do not work out we will pay your fare home. How does that sound?'

Mary smiled broadly in reply.

'Oh, and Mary, please supply me with the telephone numbers of two people who can give you a character reference.'

Mary had not been expecting to be asked for two referees. She suddenly remembered the florist shop. She had simply forgotten to go to work, so obsessed had she been with getting Rose to lend her Marty, with getting out of the situation in the flat. She could not give the florist shop manageress as a referee. She heard herself mention Susannah from the agency and regretted it immediately. Susannah knew Simon and probably Hartley, too. She'll know all about me by now. Oh, why did I say Susannah?

Mrs Mercer got to her feet. Mary got up too, and still carrying Marty, showed her to the door.

' You won't be lonely in New York,' she said. 'We have a lot of people over. You'll have some free time. You'll be able to make friends.'

Wondering what she meant, Mary bade her goodbye. What made her think I'm lonely? She thought. She had the uneasy feeling that it had something to do with the unwanted visitor from upstairs. Oh God, she thinks I encourage that sort of friendship because I'm lonely? Well at least it's better than knowing the truth.

Mary tried not to dwell on the idea that everyone in the neighbourhood knew that she was a tart. She was becoming paranoid. That no one from the shop had been to see why she had not come to work must mean that they knew. She imagined the matronly manageress asking Tim what's-his-name about her and being told lurid tales. She worried that she would not be allowed back into the States because she was an undesirable alien.

Putting Marty down on his bedding on the floor, Mary looked around for a drink. There was none. She had not had a drink since Christmas. She wanted one. She would have to

65

phone Susannah and she could not do it sober. Marty woke up and started to cry. She picked him up and tried to soothe him. She could not take him to the off licence and she could not leave him alone in the flat. She would have to phone Susannah before Mrs Mercer got back to her hotel. She had to do it now. With Marty still whimpering in the background she dialled the number. Susannah sounded pleased to hear from her. 'I wondered what had become of you, Mary.' She said she would be pleased to give Mary a character reference 'It's perfectly reasonable for a girl to leave school and find she doesn't like office work. You are such a nice, gentle girl Mary. You'll make a perfect nanny.'

Mary didn't bother to worry if Susannah was lying. Surely she would not say something too different to Mrs Mercer. The conversation with Susannah over, she phoned Hartley to warn him about the call from Mrs Mercer. It amused her to tell Hartley what he must say, and to describe little Marty to him. 'I said he takes after you, daddy,' she said and laughed. She was laughing at Hartley and he didn't mind. 'Don't forget to sound like the proud father. I'll call you tonight our time and you must tell me everything she says about me and everything you say about me. And Hartley, she'll ask you about your wife. Just think of something to say, why she's not there. But be prepared. She may want to speak to "Mrs Hartley". Think of something and make it good.'

She wanted to tell Hartley how fond she was of him but decided against it. I am fond of him, she said to herself. She could almost say he was like a father to her. But a homosexual father who had raped her and put her on the game? No, it was too much to fathom. She picked Marty up and cradled him to her, feeling comfort from his soft little body. She would not try to fathom it.

She wanted a drink. She made coffee. Then she called Hartley back. 'Hello Hartley,' she said. 'I wanted to tell you that I am very fond of you.'

There was an embarrassed laugh at the other end of the phone, then a long pause. 'Stay in touch, Mary,' he said. 'You know where to find me if you need me.'

Mrs Mercer had promised to phone the successful applicant on Saturday morning. Mary would not have long to wait. And then she would be going to America again. Where the neighbours did not know her, where only a few lonely middle-aged expats knew her, and would have forgotten her anyway. She would be free.

She picked Marty up and danced with him around the flat. 'So the neighbours know I'm a tart, so the florist shop knows I'm a tart. So my family knows, so everyone in London knows, so what?' Her shouting and dancing woke Marty up who started screaming. And the sudden pungent smell told Mary that he needed changing. She did not find changing his nappy a very pleasant experience.

'I won't feed little Dan as much as I gave you today Marty,' she said, nuzzling his neck until he gurgled. She would have liked to have kept Marty for longer but she did not want to run into her mother. It was 3.45 p.m. She would have to take him back right away or Mrs Palmer would be home from work. She collected together all his new belongings and wrapped him up warmly. As she put his new woolly hat on his head she suddenly held him close to her.

'I'm your auntie, baby, your Auntie Mary, and I love you,' she said.

By the time the taxi had reached Tottenham, Marty was asleep again. Mary did not bother to get the driver to stop down the street away from her mother's house. They stopped right outside and she gave the driver a huge tip and asked him to carry all of Marty's new things to the front door. She had seen Rose looking out of the window and the astonishment on her face when she saw the taxi and all the packages.

'Well, here he is, safe and sound,' she said smiling. 'Sorry, Rosie, I can't stop, I have to get back.'

The taxi driver had started up his engine. Mary waved him to stop. 'See you soon, Rose,' she lied. Then she kissed Marty and left without looking back. For the first time in her life she did not care what people thought of her. When Mrs Mercer phoned to offer her the job, Mary was almost blasé.

9

Mary's plan was to go to New York and never come back. She wanted a new life. She wanted to be where no one knew her. Where she could start again and no one could judge her by her past. She thought of going for one last look at her father's grave. As always when she thought of her father now, Mary thought of Ruth, and she knew it was Ruth she wanted to understand most of all. She felt that if she understood why Ruth had killed herself she would understand her father and herself better, that somehow she would feel closer to her father. Why she thought this, she did not know.

What would Joyce think if I turned up now? She wondered; or John, or Harry? They had always been kind, in a distant sort of way. She knew why now. To lose a sister so young and then to lose their mother must have been very hard to bear. And then to have their father remarry so soon must have devastated them.

Mary was having disturbing dreams. She had wondered if they were in some way connected to her drinking. She did not want to start drinking again. One dream in particular had haunted her since she had learned of Ruth's death.

She was in a street listening to a street orator. He had a small crowd around him, a crowd who apparently thought he was worthy of a hearing. They seemed to think he was a good man. Suddenly the same man was twisting the arm of a frail young girl who stood with downcast eyes, compliant and uncomplaining. Then Mary saw the girl about to go through a door and tried to stop her, knowing that if she did go through the door she would not return. In desperation, Mary took off her jumper and put it around the girl, feeling the warmth of the wool on the girl's body. She tried with all her strength of will to get the girl to stay in the room but she went out through the door. And then the girl was dead, lying on a sort of chaise-longue covered with a cloth. In the shadows of the room stood Mary's mother and Mary's half sister, Joyce.

Mary always woke up from the dream crying. She *had* to ask her mother about Ruth. She had connected this dream with Ruth, though it seemed to make little sense. If I knew more about Ruth, then I would understand, and then I might stop having the dream, she thought.

Mrs Palmer was alone when Mary went to the house. She seemed almost cheerful. 'We wondered when you would turn up again, Mary,' she said. 'Don't worry, I won't ask you where you've been or where you got those nice clothes from. I wouldn't get the truth anyway.'

'Mum, I want to ask you something important,' said Mary. 'I want to ask you about Dad's other daughter, about Ruth.'

'Oh, yes, I wondered when you'd get round to that. Joyce had no right to tell Rose about her, it's none of our business.'

'But Rose didn't tell me, Mum. How long has Rose known?'

'Oh, she met Joyce in Tesco's and went home with her. Her Sylvia is getting married and they have asked us, though I won't go. Will you go?' For some reason Mrs Palmer seemed to find this idea funny. 'She told Rose, but she had no business to. It's not our business. You can't go raking things up.'

'But she killed herself,' cried Mary. 'Dad must have been so upset. Why were there no photographs of her? Why was I never told about her?'

'You, you, you it's always *you*,' said Mrs Palmer. 'It was nothing to do with *you*. You always want to know everything. It does no good.'

'She was my sister, too.'

'*Your* sister,' said Mrs Palmer. 'You've got a sister. You've got Rose, and much you care about her. You go off and never trouble about your own sister. Then you come here trying to rake up the past which is nothing to do with you.'

'I'm going to America to live, Mum,' said Mary. 'I don't know when I'll be back.'

Mrs Palmer let out a long breath and made as if to speak. Then she pursed her lips. 'Well, your Uncle Pete is coming around in a minute. Stay and see him.'

Mary looked hard at her mother at the mention of Uncle Pete. That settled it. If this woman thought she could bear to face that man, then the chasm between them was too great. She would have to go and see Joyce. With only a few days to go before getting on the plane with Mrs Mercer, Mary decided to go straight round to see her half-sister.

Joyce looked surprised when she opened the door, then suspicious. Mary wondered what Rose had told her. She supposed that anyone who suddenly seems to have a lot of money at such a young age would arouse suspicion. She sat on the edge of the sofa drinking tea and wondering how she could bring the conversation around to Ruth.

Joyce was chattering on about the forthcoming wedding of her daughter. She said she hoped Mary would be able to come, too. 'But you've never really been a family girl, have you, Mary? We often wondered what you were thinking about, you always seemed to be somewhere else.'

'I was wondering,' Mary stopped. How could she broach this now? It seemed cruel. 'I was wondering, have you got any photos of when you were young?' The suspicion snapped back into Joyce's eyes.

'That's a funny question,' she said slowly.

Mary tried to sound casual. 'Oh, I haven't got any of Dad and I'm going away, I didn't like to take Mum's,' she said.

'Going away?' Joyce sniffed loudly and lit a cigarette, narrowing her eyes.

Mary wondered what she had been told. Did everyone know she had been on the game? Had her mother assumed that about her when she found Hartley's money in her purse? It must have been an assumption. How would they know? Just because she seemed to have some money? Did they think she was a prostitute, just because she travelled by taxi? The thought suddenly made her laugh. Oh shit, she thought, I'm fed up with this.

'Joyce,' she said in a voice louder than she had intended.

Joyce immediately looked guarded. 'Joyce, I've asked Mum and she says it is none of my business, but Ruth was my sister, too.'

For a minute Joyce looked as if she had been slapped in the face.

'Ruth,' she said. 'All this is because you want some photos of Ruth? So that's why you've come. I thought it was funny, you coming to see me.'

Joyce was hostile now and Mary decided not to stay for long. She would look at the album her half-sister had gone to fetch and then she would leave. There were the usual snaps of children in school uniform, on holiday, with the dog; nothing very interesting. Mary gazed at the photos of the younger version of her father. He looked happier in his first marriage than she remembered him. But, she told herself, Ruth was still alive then.

One photograph caught her attention. Three figures: her dad smiling straight at the camera, the slight figure of Ruth next to him with wind-blown fair hair and a serious look, and then Joyce next to her, looking at her sister with a frown. Just that, looking at her sister with a frown. For some reason Mary felt this was significant, that it went beyond normal sibling rivalry. That it had something to do with their father. She shivered and decided against asking for any photographs.

No, a clean break, she thought. It suddenly felt claustrophobic in the room. Joyce had smoked numerous cigarettes, and was not one to open windows; maybe it was that. Mary made her goodbyes to a now openly smirking Joyce, who called after her from the front door: 'Don't forget to ask us to *your* wedding, Mary,' and then laughed.

10

Mary's new life, though hard work, felt like a holiday after her experience since leaving school only, she realised with surprise, just over six months before. She had sole charge of the children, four-year-old Martha and two-year-old Dan, getting up when they did and bathing them, fixing their breakfast and eating with them, taking them out or reading to them, and hearing Martha read. Martha was a bright child who was due to go to an afternoon kindergarten in late January. Mary quickly became very fond of the kids and felt very contented. She was usually free after their bedtime at six p.m. and spent her time reading or watching television.

She remained in awe of Angela Mercer who was very kind and generous, treating Mary twice a week to afternoon tea in smart hotels and cafés where the children learned to act properly in public. Mary liked her employer's directness and felt she was liked and appreciated. Angela rarely questioned her about her family, but talked to her about the books she had read and the music she liked.

Mary felt less comfortable with Angela's husband, Michael, a lawyer, who was rather cool towards her. Neither could she find much common ground with the friends who regularly came to dinner. Mary was never required to do any cooking or preparation since Angela always had outside caterers take care of everything when they had guests, cooking for herself and Michael when they did not. A cleaner came three times a week.

Mary was content to get to know the children. Both were bright and talkative, constantly asking questions about Mary's family, about London and most of all about her accent.

Martha did not think it sounded like a real British accent. She demonstrated a real British accent as something out of an old fashioned movie, full of 'Oh, I says', and 'Don't you knows', which made them all giggle uncontrollably.

'Mine is a London accent,' laughed Mary. 'I don't talk posh.'

'Posh, what's that?' asked Dan.

'It's the way rich people speak. Kings and queens, dukes and duchesses, people like that.'

The kids were very amused at the idea of kings, queens, dukes and duchesses, and walked around the kitchen with saucepans on their heads, talking 'posh British'. They made Mary wear a saucepan, too.

Angela rarely got up before eleven a.m. and was out most afternoons. At least once a week she met Michael for dinner in a hotel in Manhattan, and they usually spent what she called a romantic night there. Mary did not mind being left alone in the apartment. It felt very secure with its entryphone system and friendly team of porters, who always raised their hats to residents and visitors alike.

Angela suggested that Mary go out on her days off and make some friends. Mary said she was happy the way things were. She did not want to admit to Angela that she would find meeting strangers difficult without a drink, and she did not want to start drinking again. She wanted to keep her job. It was the most secure life she had ever known and the happiest she had ever been.

One afternoon while the children were having their nap, she phoned Hartley in London. He had inherited more than he'd expected from his father's estate and he and Anton had bought an antiques business from an old friend who had retired. Keeping on the staff to run the shop and attend to all the paperwork, they spent most of their days happily together at auctions.

'Simon and Mireille are doing very well, Mireille in particular,' said Hartley. 'You must have seen one of her films, she made two this year in quick succession. A speaking part in the second one.'

73

Mary admitted that she had not. 'I'd like to, though I can't imagine her as an actress. As long as I don't have to meet her, or Simon again, Hartley,' she said.

'You really fell for Simon, didn't you, little one?'

'Oh, I don't know that I fell for him exactly. I was totally fascinated by him at work. He was so wonderful looking, so tall and all that floppy blond hair. I was just totally besotted. I won't ever get over that feeling. But I didn't really like him. I never got to know him, anyway. He just made me weak and confused every time I saw him. I lost all common sense and did a lot of stupid things. Like losing my job over him.'

'He has that effect on a lot of people,' said Hartley.

'Oh no, not you too, Hartley! Ho, ho you *didn't*? You didn't try it on?'

Hartley was not amused. Mary laughed. 'You are funny, Hartley, I didn't mean to hurt your feelings. Simon just goes for glamour, that's all.'

'Yes, and female glamour, at that,' said Hartley. 'I missed out on both counts.'

'But Hartley, you're gorgeous. Anton loves you, and I love you. I don't know where I'd be now without you. According to the dastardly Simon, you were the best kind of pimp to have. No psycho clients, not too many drugs, and all I have to worry about is my drink problem.'

She heard a sound behind her. Just a shuffling of feet. Michael stood in the doorway. In panic, Mary looked at the clock – she had been on the phone for ages. How long had he been there? How much had he heard?

She told Angela about the phone call to London and was told that she need not pay for it: she must phone her friends at home. Mary waited for Angela to say something about what Michael may have overheard. But she just wanted to know whom Mary had been calling.

'You never seem to call your family or friends, Mary, or they you. I find that rather odd.' The statement hung in the air while Angela looked at her quizzically.

'Oh, it was, er, Hartley. Um, *Mr* Hartley,' said Mary, blushing suddenly. She felt sure Michael had heard what she had been saying at the end of the conversation and was bound to have said something to Angela about it. Given her the circumstantial evidence . . .

'How is little Marty Hartley?' said Angela looking directly at Mary until she became uncomfortable and looked away. 'He must be getting a big boy now. You must miss him. You must get Mrs Hartley to send you some photographs. Or why not bring him over?'

The question hung in the air, the silence demanding an answer. Mary stammered and looked at the floor. 'Marty Hartley' she thought, fearing she would begin to laugh hysterically. It sounded like 'Mighty Hearty' if you said it quickly. Why hadn't she thought of that? No one called Hartley would call their son Marty. She could not look Mrs Mercer in the eye. She was afraid, afraid her past was about to surface. How stupid I am to tell Angela who I was talking to, she thought. Why don't I think quickly enough? To Angela, Hartley is supposedly a middle-aged Englishman and father of Marty, who gave me a character reference. Now she must suspect something if Michael did overhear. In the silence which followed Mary prayed that Angela would not ask about Hartley's wife.

Mary imagined things were very strained after that and it made her feel very insecure. She worried constantly about giving herself away. She worried that Michael would trace the call and phone Hartley. Maybe he would get Anton who would 'give the game away'. Mary smiled grimly at her choice of word.

'Why don't you go out and meet kids your own age, Mary?' Angela urged her.

Mary felt awkward with people her own age, and did not feel able to explain that she had never had any real friends to go out with at home. It would be impossible for her to start now in a different country where she found the culture very, very different. How could she expect someone as rich, beautiful and confident as Angela to understand that? It was useless even to try. Mary preferred to be thought of as shy and awkward than the ex-drunk, ex-prostitute she actually was.

She was afraid to meet men. She would not know how to behave. She was still taking the Pill. She had found from the start that it suited her very well. She no longer got spots and her periods, previously heavy and rather painful, were now trouble-free. She had found a private doctor in New York who supplied her with a similar brand of Pill to the one she was used to. But she wanted to avoid exposing herself to the risk of a sexual encounter. She'd had enough sex for a while. She wanted a quiet life. She loved the children and looked up to Angela, thinking her the most glamorous and cultured woman she had ever met.

The Mercers' friends were all established or upwardly mobile lawyers. They were friendly to Mary, but she knew that even with her 'cute' British accent she was still just the nanny.

Angela told Mary that her mother had died the previous year and her father had taken his loss hard. Feeling awkward around the subject of illness and death, Mary did not ask how Mrs Hansen had died. Mr Hansen had been in Europe on business and was due to return soon. Angela planned a quiet dinner for him. But to the Mercers, a quiet dinner meant employing caterers and allowing the children to stay up to see their grandpa. The kids' presence meant Mary would be there, too. Angela's elder sister, Lauren, was to make up the party with her husband, Charles – yet another lawyer.

Mary was intrigued to meet Angela's family and they were all that she had expected – tall and attractive, full of confidence and exuberance. They were all very clever and witty, too, and Mary felt shy in their presence. She was glad the kids were there. They were greatly fussed over by all the adults but they insisted on including Mary in everything.

Mr Hansen was the head of a large and very successful firm of attorneys and his daughters clearly adored him. The conversation at dinner was about the theatre and literature and, of course, the law, which the entire family seemed to find fascinating.

They're an old fashioned family, thought Mary. The women left the men at the table to drink whisky and talk about the law, while Mary put the children to bed.

Mr Hansen had been very kind to Mary. She felt that he had kept trying to include her in the conversation, as the kids had. He was very distinguished-looking, with thick curly white hair, very white teeth and a friendly smile. He became a regular visitor, always taking time to talk to Mary and the children.

'How's little Miss English Rose?' he would say to her. He had been to London many times and knew it better that Mary did. It surprised him that she had never been to the theatre or the cinema in the West End; that she had spent all her life in a drab North London suburb, never really going anywhere else.

'But what did you do as a child?' he asked her. 'Didn't your dad and mom take you anywhere?'

'I suppose they worked too hard,' said Mary. She knew they must have done some things together, she remembered going to pantomimes, but she couldn't really think of much else. She felt guilty about painting such a negative picture of her family. She felt she had let them down. 'They both worked but we didn't have much money,' she said. 'And then my father died and we had even less. My mother was very sad when my father died.'

Again she thought of Ruth, but decided against telling Mr Hansen about her. She suddenly remembered Simon's face when he had seen her untidy front room at home, and faltered.

Mr Hansen began introducing her to the sons of his friends, all of whom seemed alarming to Mary. The only men she had mixed with had been Hartley's cilents. She found she could not open her mouth in the presence of clever, rising young lawyers. They seemed pretty bored in her company anyway; she overhead one of them telling Mr Hansen that she was 'Pretty all right, and pretty dumb.'

She wanted Mr Hansen to think well of her, not as someone with a sad, poverty-stricken background. She was fed up with seeing herself as a put-upon creature, she wanted to be other than a victim. She wanted to feel happy and have some fun. But she was at a loss to know how to go about it. The thought of going out with young lawyers simply alarmed her. Hoping to sound intelligent and interesting, she said: 'I thought I'd go to some art galleries and museums. There are some wonderful ones in New York, I hear,' though she had heard no such thing.

Mr Hansen looked sympathetic. 'But you can't go on your own, Mary, we must find someone to take you about a bit.'

'Oh, Angela and I go out,' said Mary, though this was no longer true. Angela had changed towards her and their outings had all but stopped.

She was getting to like Daniel Hansen. He was one of the kindest men she had ever met. He seemed decent and honest, too. It was a relief to be with someone and not feel she had to be on her guard. It did not seem apparent that Angela or Michael had said anything to him about any reservations they might be having.

'You should go out, young lady,' he said. 'A pretty kid like you should be having fun.'

'But I like being with the children,' said Mary. She wished she could get them off the subject of her going out and making friends. Where did they expect her to go? 'I'm happy the way I am, really, Mr Hansen,' she said, laughing so that he might believe that she was.

'Please, Mary, call me Daniel,' he said. 'My folks have been lawyers in New York for four generations,' he told her proudly. 'My late wife studied law, too, but she gave it up when the children were born.'

'What was your wife like?' asked Mary.

'Oh, she was smart, pretty too, like my girls. She was devoted to them. She could have been a successful lawyer, but me and the kids came first with her.' He fell silent. Mary wanted to ask why his wife had died, but did not like to. Remembering Ruth's suicide made her reticent about asking others about such things.

Daniel Hansen often called at the apartment on his way out to dine or to go to theatres or concerts. He always spent time with Mary and the children. He seemed to be very rich and Mary wondered when he actually did any legal work. He

78

employed a lot a people; she supposed he got others to do the work for him.

He arrived one evening to say a friend was unable to keep a theatre date and suggested Angela and Michael use the tickets. Angela was very disappointed: they had people coming over for dinner. The caterers were expected at 7.30 p.m. They were sitting in the kitchen and Mary had been fixing the children's supper. Suddenly Daniel said, 'Why don't I take Mary?'

Angela said hurriedly, 'No, no, Dad, that's okay. Look, I'll come with you. It's only the Petersens, we can make our excuses.'

'No, no you don't want to go cancelling them now, that won't do at all,' said her father. 'Jeff Petersen is an important man. Mary could come along with me. She can put the kids to bed. In fact, I'll help her put the kids to bed. Grandpas don't get many chances like this. Come on, Mary. He put an arm around Angela. 'Don't make that face, chicken. Why can't your old dad take a pretty girl out? She'll look after me,' he added, laughing.

Mary caught Angela's stiff expression and worried. She did not want to go out with Mr Hansen. She did not want to put another foot wrong. She needed this job and this home. She feared she would have no alternative but to go back to London, and that was no alternative. She decided she must talk to Angela. She had to find out what had gone wrong. If Michael had overheard what she'd said to Hartley, then she must try to get around it somehow. She could not allow anything to spoil this job for her. She was becoming attached to the children and could not bear to go back to an uncertain future in London.

Daniel was laughing. 'Well, that's settled then. You'll have to put up with me tonight, Mary, my dear. Don't look so worried. We'll get along fine.'

11

Daniel Hansen took to coming every day to the apartment just as Mary was fixing the kid's supper. Martha and Dan jumped up and ran to him when they saw him. They both loved their grandpa. They rode around the kitchen on his shoulders and played with his hair. He clearly loved being with them and always helped Mary put them to bed. He had a seemingly endless variety of stories to tell them.

They always wanted him to tell them about London. Had he met the king and queen? Did he meet Mary there? Was it really always grey and raining? They kept their questions up until Mary and Daniel were exhausted. Then they wanted to play a game. But there always came a point when Daniel got very firm with them and they always obeyed him and got back into bed when they could see that he was serious.

Mary envied Angela and Lauren such a dad. She wondered what their mother had been like. Since Angela did not look as much like her dad as Lauren did, Mary assumed she must take after her mother.

'You must miss her very much,' she said suddenly one evening. She realised she had been watching Daniel, seeing his evident enjoyment in his grandchildren.

He turned to look at her. 'Who, Mary?' he said, distracted for a moment by Martha, who had been tying a red ribbon in his abundant hair. Then he realised. 'Oh, yes,' he said, 'oh yes.' He smiled straight at Mary and she felt uneasy.

Mary made herself talk to Angela, asking her if everything was okay. She wanted to be reassured, hoping that nothing was wrong, but dreading that something might be. Angela looked at her for a full minute, while Mary tried in vain to return the fixed, confident look.

'We realise we know so little about you, Mary. You are kind to the kids but your inexperience is obvious. We even began to wonder just how much experience you have had. This Mr Hartley spoke very highly of you, but I'll be straight with you, Mary. Michael heard you on the phone to this Mr Hartley. He said it was a very odd conversation. What sort of man is he?'

'Oh, he makes jokes,' said Mary. 'He's harmless. He doesn't take life very seriously.'

She had a dead feeling in the pit of her stomach. She dreaded what was coming. Please, please, Angela, she was pleading silently, please don't say any more. Please don't send me back to London. Her mind was racing. Had Michael heard the word 'pimp'? Did it mean the same in America? Had he heard her say she had a drink problem?

'Also,' Angela was saying, 'my father is a very kind man, but he misses my mom. Please don't read anything into his friendship with you. He is just a very kind man.'

Mary was shocked. 'Of course not, he's your father,' she said. 'I like to see him and he loves being with the kids. But I don't read anything into it. He took me to the theatre that night because there was no one else for him to take.'

'We'll say no more for now,' said Angela.

When Daniel arrived as usual the next evening, Angela told him that she and Michael would be taking him out to dinner and he must be ready to go as soon as the kids were in bed. Mary knew this would leave him no time to talk to her and was relieved. Now perhaps it would all blow over. She simply wanted to be left alone until she felt more in control of her life.

The next evening, Angela and Michael together made it clear to Mary that while they knew it was an innocent friendship, they felt it did not look well for Mr Hansen to be so much in the company of a girl more than 30 years his junior. Mary wondered who else could possibly know about her friendship with Daniel. They had been to the theatre together once. Mary wondered if the Mercers imagined something had

81

happened between herself and Daniel the evening they went out. And again she wondered if they knew about her past.

'Your father is a very kind, gentlemanly man . . .' Her voice began to shake, she felt a rising anger. They were talking to her as if she was not good enough for them. She had been out with him *once*. He did not come to see her, he came to see *their* kids. 'I have never encouraged him. He was kind to me and that is all. I would not want it any other way,' she said. To her annoyance she found that she had started to cry. She was angry with herself for letting them upset her, and childishly annoyed at Angela for wanting to keep her precious father to herself.

Unusually, it was Michael who spoke first. 'Of course, of course, Mary,' he said. 'We're not trying to make anything of this. But you must see that it looks odd. A man of fifty and a seventeen-year-old girl.'

Angela recovered herself. Mary could not understand why she should be so upset. Daniel had not for one moment made any kind of suggestion that he was 'dating' her. He came to see his grandkids. It seemed to Mary that Angela had been disproportionately upset.

'We're not accusing you, Mary. Look, let us leave it at that. We'll talk in a couple of weeks when your three months are up.'

Feeling herself dismissed, Mary left to go to her room. As she closed the door she heard Angela's voice: 'Michael, he's besotted with her. And what do we really know about her?'

Mary listened at the door. Michael said: 'We agreed we would let things sit. The kids love Mary and she's good with them. I thought you liked the girl.'

'Yes, you're right,' said Angela. 'She's a good kid. I suppose she was just joking with this Mr Hartley. But it seems an odd joke for a kid like that to make.'

'We could check this Hartley guy out,' said Michael. 'If there's a problem your dad will understand. He's just flattered that Mary likes him. She's a very pretty girl.'

'I think it's more than that. He's lonely, Mike,' she said. 'I'm afraid he'll make a fool of himself over her.'

82

Michael laughed and put his arms around his wife. 'He should find someone his own age and marry again,' he said.

Angela pulled away from him. 'No, no, Michael, no,' she said. 'Mom's only been gone a year. They loved each other so much. He would never, never want to be with anyone else.'

'It's all right, baby,' said Michael, pulling her close to him. 'We'll talk to him again. He's agreed he'll look a damn fool being seen around with a common little nanny at his age.'

Mary did not know what to do. She liked Daniel and missed his company. But she was relieved not to have the problem of Angela's daily disapproval. She could not believe she had been right that Mr Hansen was 'besotted' with her. He was a rich, handsome and clever lawyer. It did not seem likely.

She thought of looking for other nanny jobs. Maybe Angela would feel happier if she left. But she did not want to leave the kids, who were already fretting about their grandpa whom they had not seen for three days.

She was in the kitchen with Angela trying to find the right words to broach the subject when Daniel suddenly arrived at the door. He said he wanted to speak to Mary alone. Angela protested but he insisted.

'I've tried, Mary, but I can't put you out of my mind,' said Daniel. 'I've never met anyone like you. So sweet and unspoiled, so funny and smart. Please say that you will consider marrying me.'

'I can't marry you!' cried Mary. The idea seemed ludicrous to her. 'I like you, but I can't marry you.' She thought of Angela and the kids; everyone would think it a crazy idea. She felt no one would accept them. Finally she decided Daniel must be joking.

Angela came into the room. 'Dad,' she said. She was crying. Mary realised she must have heard what her father had said and left the room at once. She wanted above all to stay on good terms with Angela. She wanted a reference for another job. She wanted to be able to go on seeing Martha and Dan.

But it was too late. Angela was now openly hostile towards her. She mentioned Mr Hartley again, asking if he and his wife ever came back to the States, asking exactly what Mr Hartley did for a living.

'Angela, would you be happier if I got another job? I'm very fond of you and the kids; I don't want to lose that. I like Daniel, but of course I'm not right for him.'

Angela's face hardened.

'Please, Angela, we've got along well. I want us to be friends. Let me find another job,' she pleaded. 'I could find another job in New York and still see the kids. I need not bump into Mr Hansen again.'

She was afraid that Angela already knew about Hartley, already knew about her past occupation. She did not want to hear this confirmed. She just wanted to leave as soon as she could find another job. Angela said she would speak to Michael and it was agreed that Mary could stay until they found another nanny. The whole episode upset the children who were used to Mary. Angela went to see her father to tell him that it was all for the best. 'Mary will get another job. She is a good nanny. The kids love her, but they miss you, Dad,' she said. 'When she goes, everything will get back to normal, you'll see.'

Daniel insisted he had fallen in love with Mary and he wasn't going to change his mind about her. 'I love her. I intend to ask her again to be my wife,' he said. 'I intend to marry her, Angela.'

Mary had a couple of interviews but got nervous when asked why she was leaving the Mercers' employ after such a short time. She did badly, and was not offered a job. She realised just how much Angela must have taken her on face value, just seeing her with Marty. I am a calculating bitch, she told herself. I set up the whole thing. I am calculating and dishonest, and soon they will all know it, if they don't already. How could I have been so stupid?

The prospective employers in New York wanted references from London as well as from the Mercers. Mary knew that Hartley would do what he could, but what if they checked him out? Americans (and particularly lawyers) seemed very keen on checking people out. She had heard that companies even vetted the wives of prospective employees. They had the means to do it. She was more and more convinced that the Mercers knew everything about her relationship with Hartley.

Angela found a replacement nanny quite quickly and suggested to Mary that the best course of action would be to pay her fare home as had been agreed, and as soon as possible. Feeling that the alternative might be the exposure of her past life, Mary agreed. By the next morning the flight to London had been booked and Mary's bags were packed and ready to go to the airport. Angela had taken the children to spend the previous night with Lauren and Charles. They had been told that Mary had to return to London to see her mother. Mary could only ask Angela to say she promised to write to them. She had not been given the chance to say goodbye. She feared that Angela would not explain things to the children and that they would think she had just left them.

She had tried to call Hartley at his flat but got no reply. She would just have to turn up and hope that he would be there; she no longer had the keys. She hoped that he would not mind. She would have to ask him if she could stay there until she found a job. She remembered the last time she had turned up unannounced at his home. What is it with you, she said to herself, that people keep throwing you out? She found herself laughing. But she had to will herself not to cry. Perhaps it was better this way. At least she had escaped the humiliation of the Mercers confronting her with the past. She could only hope they had not gone so far as to investigate Hartley. She felt powerless and silly. She was being dismissed again without a chance to explain. Angela just wanted her dad to herself, she thought. I wasn't doing them any harm.

She felt sure Daniel could not really have fallen in love with her, that he would have got over his infatuation or whatever it was eventually and things would have been all right, if only they had let her stay long enough to get another job. But it was too late now.

She looked at Angela's perfect profile as they rode to the airport together in the back of a taxi. Mrs Mercer sat motionless, no expression on her face.

'If it's because of your father, Angela . . .' Mary began in a faltering voice.

Angela turned to look at her, holding her gaze for what seemed like an eternity. 'You are very pretty, Mary, and you have a certain quality that makes you easy to be with. You don't judge or criticise, I suppose that's what it is. My Dad is very lonely right now. I suppose he thought you would be a diversion for him.' She suddenly became agitated. 'But my Mother has just died.' Here her voice faltered and tears began to fall. 'They loved each other *so* much. People would think him a fool if he suddenly married again. Especially if he married someone thirty years younger. Thirty years, Mary. People would think you were a little gold digger making a fool of a lonely man.'

'I had no intention of marrying him,' said Mary. 'I thought we would just be on friendly terms because of the kids. I mean, he liked me, we had fun playing with the kids. He's great with them and they love him. That's how I saw it. I didn't know he was going to ask me to marry him. I promise you I didn't. I knew I was just the nanny. I didn't encourage him.'

She did not hear Angela's reply, which was muffled by tears. Mary was relieved Angela had not mentioned Hartley. Maybe that meant she had not checked him out. Thank God, thought Mary. She tried to amuse herself by imagining walking into the florist shop and asking for her job back. That job seemed like heaven compared to what was happening to Mary now – being escorted from the premises yet again.

She wished she had never met Mrs Mercer. I can never be a nanny again, she told herself sadly. It's too painful to leave the children. Mary felt angry and resentful. It's not fair, she thought. What chance did Rose and I have? Why did my Dad have to be so old? Why did he have to die?

They had two hours to wait before Mary's flight was called. Angela got some coffee for them and they sat down to wait in silence. The waiting and silence became unbearable. Mary wanted to get up and walk about, anything but sit with the silent, brooding Angela. Both were close to tears. Finally Mary said: 'Look, don't wait with me Angela.'

Angela did not speak for a moment and Mary imagined she suspected she would not get on the plane if left to herself.

'My luggage is checked in. I only have my passport and tickets. I have very little money. Don't worry. I won't do a runna.' she said. Angela smiled, unexpectedly amused at this quaint piece of Londonese.

'I know you wouldn't do that, Mary,' she said. 'I'm sorry, I just didn't want to leave you here by yourself.'

'No, no, I'd rather,' said Mary. 'I'll walk about and get a magazine. I can't sit here. I just can't.' She was afraid she was going to cry. 'I liked you, I thought we would get on well. I'm sorry this happened. I didn't want it to happen.'

'I know, Mary, I'm sorry, too. Will you really be all right if I leave?'

'Yes,' said Mary. 'It seems to get harder the longer you stay.' They got to their feet and Angela gave Mary a hug.

'Look after yourself Mary. I know you will be all right. Look, you're a bright kid. Why don't you go back and graduate, or whatever it is you do in England? You could do well for yourself. You're too sentimental to be a nanny. You're probably too sentimental to be a mother also.'

Mary was glad to be alone. She walked slowly toward the bookstall to look at the magazines. She had a wild idea that she would sell her ticket and stay in New York. But where would she stay until she found a job? It was impossible. She reached for a magazine with a picture of the Beatles on the front of it. She was out of touch with what was going on at home. It surprised her that they had become so popular in the States. She liked the Beatles but they were nowhere near as good as The Who.

She suddenly heard Daniel's voice say her name. She turned to see him smiling at her. 'I waited for Angela to go,' he said. 'Mary, I've come to take you home.'

21

Daniel had been to see Lauren and heard of the plan to send Mary away. Despite her reluctance to betray the sisters' plans, Lauren had told her father when Mary's flight was due to leave. She could not in the end defy her father. She shared her sister's opposition to her dad marrying again. It seemed disloyal to both of them that he should fall in love with someone else, and especially someone so young. That she was a nanny made it seem much, much worse. They had expected Mr Hansen to come to his senses once Mary had gone.

Lauren could not stop him from running after Mary, but she did not believe he would go through with the marriage. The worst she thought would happen was that Mary would stay a little longer and that her father would see what a mistake he was making. Her departure would just be delayed.

Daniel wished the marriage to take place very soon. In the meantime, Mary was to live with the family of an old family friend in New England. This was an awkward time for Mary. She had been relieved that Daniel had wanted to wait until they were married before they slept together. She wanted to wait. It would be a relief to sleep with someone she had got to know first. And Daniel was so gentlemanly and kind she was not worried about it. She was aware that she was very lucky indeed to be marrying such a rich man.

But his friends did not seem to know what to say to her. They seemed embarrassed by her presence, either rushing around trying to organise things to keep her amused, or pointedly 'leaving her to herself'. She did not know what to say to them, and there were long silences. She felt like a prisoner in their house. It all seemed unreal to Mary. She

88

wished she could call Hartley but after the last time she did not dare in case she was overheard. She wondered what he would make of this new development. She imagined a jokey conversation. 'One minute, I'm talking to my ex-pimp on the phone, I'm overheard and they try to run me out of the country. The next, I'm marrying a respected fifty-year-old attorney who is richer than all the people you know put together, Hartley. Don't expect me to speak to you now.' She wished she could really talk to Hartley; she felt that he was her only friend.

She saw Daniel each evening and they were very relaxed in each other's company. He put no pressure on her. She could talk and laugh with him and didn't mind if he teased her. His teasing reminded her of Simon. She felt happy with him. He told her that Angela and Lauren were coming around to the idea of their marriage and Martha and Dan were longing to see her again. She laughed and said she didn't think this very likely. 'They think you're marrying too soon after their mother died, and I don't blame them,' she said.

Daniel took her in his arms and kissed her gently. 'I can't help it, my darling, he said. 'I love you. We must be married. Nothing else will do. They'll come around.'

Mary had not imagined falling in love again after Simon and thought in any case her choice of husband would be limited. She could not help thinking of Rose's Dave. She felt herself to be extraordinarily lucky. Daniel was fun to be with, he was kind and gentle. She had nothing to worry about. He told her that he had invented all the dinner and theatre dates he was supposed to be going on so he could call at the apartment to see her. 'I fell in love with you almost at first sight,' he said. 'I thought I was making a fool of myself. So I tried to get you to go out with young men. You never showed any interest. All you cared about was the kids. I knew then you would make the perfect wife.'

Mary had seen Angela and Michael on only two occasions since the sudden change in her fortunes. They had gone out to dinner and Mary was saddened that the children had not been included. She worried that she would not be able to see them after she had married their grandfather. Angela and Michael were polite but there was little warmth. They did not even mention Martha and Dan and Mary did not like to. She spoke very little.

Only Daniel was exuberant. He told Mary that they would come around to the idea of the marriage. 'They miss Alicia, their mother,' he said. 'We're a very close family. I didn't expect to fall in love again. But I want to make a new start. They'll come around.'

Angela had not mentioned her sister either and Mary worried that a rift might have developed between them. Had it not been for Lauren, Mary would have left for London as planned. She began to be apprehensive about the wedding, which was now only a few days away. It was to be a very simple ceremony with only close family and friends.

Daniel had asked Mary if she wanted anyone from home to attend, offering to fly them all over. Mary remembered Joyce's sarcastic comment, flung from the doorway of her house, as her own daughter was about to be married. 'Don't forget to invite us to *your* wedding, Mary.' She briefly pictured the grim little party they would make, her mother and her Uncle Pete. Rose, now pregnant again, and little Marty, and Joyce and her family, and hurriedly closed her mind to them all.

'I don't get on well with my family, Daniel,' she said. 'I would rather not ask them.'

'But why not, darling?' he said. 'I cannot understand why you don't get along with them.'

'It's since my Dad died, the family sort of fell apart when my Dad died,' she said. She wanted to tell him about Ruth, but could not. She looked so sad that Daniel did not press her further.

'You're too sensitive, Mary,' he said. 'You don't have to worry about families getting along. Things always work out, you know. There is nothing that cannot be gotten over.'

Mary knew he was referring to his own daughters and their attitude towards her but she did not dare say so. She looked closely at his face, the broad jaw and smiling mouth, the grey-green eyes and wonderfully thick white hair. He smiled back at her until she shyly said, 'You're so good-looking, Daniel. You could have anyone you wanted. I can't believe you want to marry me.'

He just laughed at her. She realised she looked up to him as someone way above her. She had never even asked herself if she loved him. He had wanted to marry her and had rescued her from being sent back to London. He was someone she admired and found it easy to be with. She suddenly realised she had not even tried to imagine what sex would be like with him. She worried that something was bound to go wrong.

She would have liked to ask Hartley to her wedding. But how would she explain that Mrs Hartley and Marty could not be with him? She amused herself by imagining getting Rose to lend Marty to Hartley, or even coming with him and pretending to be his wife. Now that really would be funny, she thought, my sister and Hartley pretending to be husband and wife, and she smiled.

'That's better, darling, you look happier now. It is going to be all right, my dear. We'll have a quiet honeymoon. It's all arranged and you'll love it. There'll be nobody else around and you'll be able to relax.' He put his arms around her. 'We *will* be all right, Mary,' he said.

Oh God, he thinks I'm worried about the wedding night, she thought. He thinks I'm a virgin. He thinks I'm worried about having sex for the first time. She felt guilty and ashamed. Maybe she should have gone back to London. What would he think if he found out? What if he knew immediately that it wasn't her first time? She knew that Angela and Michael could still check up on her background. She would never be safe.

The wedding had been planned by Daniel's PA. After the marriage service there was to be a quite, informal reception at an hotel. The only guests were to be Angela and Michael, Lauren and Charles and four of the partners in Daniel's company with their wives. Happily for Mary, Martha and Dan were to be there with their new nanny.

Mary felt that there was at least a temporary truce at the

wedding. Angela and Lauren were nice to her, complementing her on her outfit. Charles and Michael were rather cool, but Mary was glad of that; she had never known what to say to either of them. Martha and Dan were delighted to see her again.

'Where have you been? Mom said you went to stay with Lauren. But we've got Janey now, and she's from England, too, and she isn't posh like you weren't.'

The new nanny was a very talkative Liverpudlian who swore to the children that she knew the Beatles personally. She said she could get their autographs the next time she went home. She said everyone in Liverpool knew them, they were always out and about and would talk to everyone. All of her cousins had been to school with them. Martha and Dan wanted to meet them when they came to New York and Janey said she would arrange it.

Janey regarded Mary curiously. She was about two years older and had been a nanny in New York for three years. Mary noted that the Mercers had gone for experience this time. They had learned their lesson. She started worrying again. I daren't put a foot wrong, she thought. It wouldn't take much for them to find out about me and Hartley.

Janey was pulling a face at her. 'Hey, Mary, wake up,' she said. 'You were miles away.' Before Mary could answer she said, 'Why haven't your family come to your wedding? If it were me they'd need a footy stadium. Don't they approve of you marrying someone so old?'

'Oh, I don't have much family,' said Mary. 'They couldn't get away.' She felt embarrassed. This girl seemed so worldly. She feared Janey could see right through her. 'I don't think of Daniel as old. I've never really gone out with boys of my own age.' This drew an arch look from Janey, who, Mary felt. clearly saw her as a gold-digger.

'Well,' Janey said, 'I suppose if you're looking for a quiet life you could do a lot worse. They say he's hardly been out since his wife died. And he's loaded.' She shrieked with laughter suddenly. 'I mean he's rich. I keep forgetting, "loaded" means something else here. I think it's me who's

92

loaded.' Mary didn't know what she meant by that but she laughed anyway. 'I suppose you're going to have lots of children,' said Janey.

'Er, oh, I don't know,' said Mary. How had she not thought of this, either? What is wrong with me, she chided herself. I can only think of one thing at a time. But her next thought was that Daniel was unlikely to want to have children at his age. He had his grandchildren, after all.

She had been taking the Pill religiously, and it had not occurred to her to stop. She felt so much better and did not want her bad skin and painful periods to return. Maybe she should have mentioned to Daniel that she was on the Pill? She decided she had better tell him, he would understand if she said it was prescribed to stop her getting spots and painful periods. She had heard of others taking the Pill for this reason.

Janey was staring at her again. 'Mary, where do you keep going?' she said, in a voice which was rather too loud. 'I'm talking to you and you seem to be somewhere else. What are you thinking about?' She started to laugh again. 'Oh, don't look so worried. Are you pregnant already?'

'Oh, no, no I'm not,' said Mary. 'We haven't . . .' she stopped suddenly. Janey was looking at her with raised eyebrows. She took a big swig from her glass of wine. She had put away several already.

'You haven't what? Oh Jeesus, you don't mean you haven't done it?'

Mary had not drunk any wine other than one glass of champagne during the toasts. She was longing for the reception to be over. She wanted to be alone with Daniel, away from all these people, staring at her, finding conversation with her hard going. And now, she realised, wondering if she was pregnant. She looked at Janey, taking her in properly for the first time.

She was a tall, well-built girl with long, straight brown hair and a wide, smiling mouth. She talked constantly, and Mary suddenly realised, was getting quite drunk. Daniel had already said that he did not approve of Angela's too-hurried choice of a nanny. He worried that the kids might pick up bad language. And, he said, she smoked. But Mary liked her. She seemed very open and honest, and her apparent sudden suspicion that Daniel was 'doing the right thing' by marrying someone he had made pregnant seemed genuine.

Mary smiled. 'Oh no, Daniel wanted us to wait,' she said.

'Jeeesus,' said Janey. She moved closer to Mary and said in a loud whisper: 'What if it's awful? What if he can't, you know. How old is he?'

'He's only fifty,' said Mary.

'Fifty, well he is good-looking, I suppose,' said Janey. 'But, well, I hope you know what you're doing. Suppose he has some funny ideas he hasn't told you about? You never know with these rich old guys who can buy anything they want.'

Mary could hardly tell her that she had already been on the receiving end of many of the funny ideas a 50-year-old might get. Marriage to Daniel would be easy in comparison. She suddenly felt relaxed and happy, and laughed.

'I'll be fine, she said. 'I've never been one for going out much. He's very kind and I, yes I do, love him. He's good-natured; he never loses his temper, or shouts or anything. He is just a kind man. We're going to be fine.' She suddenly wanted to be with Daniel. She didn't care about the other people there any longer. Feeling a sudden warmth for the friendly girl, she said, 'You must come and see us, and bring the kids. I miss them so much.'

'Oh, right, yes, we'll come and see you,' said Janey. 'I'd like somewhere else to take them. But I don't thing Daniel likes me much. Never mind, I'll come during the day when he's at work. It'll be great.'

Mary was still smiling when she felt Daniel's arms around her shoulders. It's time for us to go, baby,' he said. He smiled rather frostily at Janey and drew Mary away.

'See you soon, Janey,' smiled Mary.

'I don't want you to encourage that girl,' said Daniel. 'She's not a good influence. I must talk to Angela about her.'

'Oh, she's all right,' said Mary. 'I quite like her, and the kids like her, too.'

'You see good in everyone, that's why I love you,' said Daniel. 'But I think we could do a lot better than that young woman for Martha and Dan.'

Angela took Mary's hands in hers and wished her every happiness. 'Janey is great,' Mary said to her when Daniel was out of earshot. 'She'll be great fun for the kids. She said she'd bring them around to see me. Is that all right with you?'

'Yes, of course,' said Angela. 'Mary, I don't mean to be . . .' She stopped herself. Mary could see that she was moved.

'I know, Angela,' she said. 'If it had been my mother that had died I would have hated my dad marrying anyone else. I won't take him away, I promise. I hope you'll come and see us, often.'

13

Mary had been nervous during the ceremony. She had felt like an impostor, standing beside Daniel in a new dress, high heels and, worst of all, a hat – the first time she had worn one. The unfamiliar formality of the clothes made her nervous. They were not a particularly jolly party. Only Daniel, smiling broadly, looked as if he was happy to be there.

Mary stumbled over her own name. 'I Mary Jennifer Pa . . ., Pa . . .' She could not say the name. The registrar smiled indulgently and Mary but her lip. She looked up at Daniel on her right. He squeezed her hand and suddenly winked. She was startled. She had never seen him wink before. He was smiling at her. As he winked, she felt a sudden, unexpected sexual charge. It was the moment she was often to remember. The moment when, looking back, she knew she wanted him.

The honeymoon was spent in New England. It was the happiest time in Mary's life. She knew Daniel wanted her and she wanted him yet still he put no pressure on her. They sat on the veranda on their first night watching the sun go down while he talked about his childhood. He had been brought up in New England and he loved being there.

She did not let herself think that he was expecting her to be a virgin. Why she could not have invented just one boyfriend from her life in London to explain away her non-virginity, she did not know. That would have been so easy. Surely one boyfriend would not have been so bad? But he had never asked her about boyfriends, he had just tested her on various young men and noted that she was not interested. He thinks of me as the dutiful nanny type, she smiled to herself. The next minute a thought struck her: Oh God, blood! He'll be expecting blood! And if there is no blood he'll know. She remembered the blood with Mick and Stu and found herself thinking fondly of them. It had been fun. But what could she do about it now?

She remembered reading in a novel that women in the Middle Ages, who should have been virgins but were not, used to take a pin (she thought it was a pin) to bed with them on their wedding night to make themselves bleed. Then there would be some blood on the bedding. But surely a pin would not cause very much blood? Certainly nowhere near as much as Mick and Stu. She began to feel tense. She took her Pill in the bathroom and then put the pack in its hiding place in her make-up bag. She had chosen a very chaste-looking nightdress. Daniel had said that he would be very gentle, that he would make love to her very gently. It *will* be the first time, in a way, she told herself. It will be the first time anyone has *made love* to me, at least. But she was afraid. Afraid of being found out. That something would happen and that he would stop loving her. That she would have to go back to London in disgrace. She must be very careful.

Daniel finished his brandy. Mary had drunk very little. She felt she did not need a drink with Daniel. I won't have to perform, she thought. I can just lie here and look as if I don't know what to do. She smiled to herself at her little joke. And then she realised it was true. This was a new experience for her. She really did not know what to do.

Daniel went into the bathroom to clean his teeth. He had put on some soft classical piano music Mary had not heard before.

'What's this, Daniel?' she asked when he came back to the bedroom.

'It's Brahms, darling,' he replied.

'The one who wrote the lullaby,' she said and he laughed.

'Yes,' he said gently, 'the one who wrote the lullaby.'

Daniel and Mary rarely went out. They were happy to be together. 'Angela and Lauren have accepted us now, as husband and wife,' said Daniel. 'I told you they would. They can see that we are happy together and everything is fine.'

Mary had to admit that this seemed to be true. They all had dinner together at least once every two weeks and there never seemed to be a problem. She knew she had lost any chance of having Angela as a friend, that could not be, but it appeared that Daniel was right. Both Angela and Lauren seemed genuinely happy for their dad. They would still talk about their mother but this did not bother Mary. She felt so grateful to Daniel, she could not imagine what would have happened to her if she had not married him.

Martha and Dan were now very close to Janey. Janey herself seemed to be the only person who could rile Daniel. He hated her accent, her smoking, her boyfriends and her self-assurance. But he gave up insisting that Angela replace her when he saw how good she was with the children. He told Mary he understood that it would not be right to cause any more disruption in their young lives. He said he would not mind if Janey came to the apartment during the day, since it meant Mary could see the children more often. Finally he had to admit to Mary that Janey had a good heart. 'I just wish she was not so, so forward,' he said.

Mary laughed at him and said he was living in the Dark Ages. 'That doesn't make her a bad person. She's young, after all, why shouldn't she be forward, whatever that means.'

'Listen to you,' said Daniel, laughing. 'You're younger than she is. But you would never behave like that.'

'Like what?' asked Mary.

'Haven't you seen the way she flirts with Charles and Michael?' he said. 'It isn't right. She should be careful; people will get the wrong idea about her. She may have a good heart, I will grant you that. But Mary, she is a tease. She behaves like a little whore.'

Mary fell silent and suddenly felt angry with Daniel. What did he know? He knew nothing.

*

October 7th was Daniel's fifty-first birthday. He had never been one for birthdays, he said, and 51 was not something to celebrate. It was also the six-month anniversary of their marriage and he wanted to do something special to mark that. They decided to go back to the house in New England for their double celebration. It was a lovely place to be during the fall and still warm enough to sit on the veranda. Daniel had more brandies than usual and was becoming sentimental. They sat in the dusk; Daniel with his head in Mary's lap, and Mary felt she could not feel more secure and contented than this.

'We should have children, darling,' Daniel said. 'I was hoping you would be pregnant by now. A child now would make everything perfect.'

Mary opened her eyes. He had spoiled the moment for her but she did not say so. Had he been hoping all this time that she would get pregnant? It had never occurred to her. He had never mentioned it. Why had he never mentioned it? Was that why he married her?

'You would make the best mother in the world, I knew that when I saw you with Martha and Dan,' he said.

'You sentimental old thing,' she replied. 'That's the brandy making you say that. I don't think I'd make the best mother in the world. I'm not eighteen.'

'Yes, you would, my darling,' he said. 'It's good to have your children young. And we should start right now.'

He got up and gently raised her to her feet. She forgot about the Pill.

The next morning Daniel slept late. When Mary woke up it was the first thing she thought of: I didn't take the Pill. She lay very still, trying to sort out her confused feelings. Would it be all right, having a baby? It would make Daniel happy. But not now, she thought. I'm not eighteen till next month. Not now. She wished she could tell Daniel she did not want a baby yet. He had said nothing about wanting to have children before they got married. She supposed he had just thought it would happen naturally, that he didn't even have to mention it. How could she tell him now that she had been on the Pill all the time? Why does he want a baby now? she thought resentfully. He has Angela and Lauren, he has Martha and Dan.

She walked slowly into the bathroom and looked at herself in the mirror. 'I may already be pregnant,' she said aloud. It would be nice to have a baby, wouldn't it? It would make Daniel happy. But Angela would hate her. Somehow she knew Angela and possibly Lauren, too, would hate her. She remembered Rose, trying to cope with Marty at eighteen. But I have Daniel, she thought, it will be all right. She looked at herself in the mirror and felt an uneasy feeling that was inexplicably turning to fear. She found her make-up bag and hurriedly swallowed a Pill. Was it too late? She tried to remember what that horrible nurse back in London had said to her.

'Don't forget to take it, ever, but if you do, take one as soon as you remember it next day.' Mary got a glass of water and drank it quickly, then she got another one and drank that, too. Then she got another Pill and swallowed it.

14

'Mary, I think you should see Doctor Schaeffer,' said Daniel. 'It's almost a year now and you haven't got pregnant. There will be something very simple he will be able to fix.'

Mary had been dreading this. Lauren had just had a son. Another bloody little lawyer, thought Mary. Though Daniel did not mention it often it had become increasingly clear that he wanted children. Most of all he wanted a son. He loved his daughters but Mary was beginning to think he had married again because he wanted a son to carry on his name. A sort of arrogance had made him choose someone he saw as young and unspoiled.

It seemed to Mary that Lauren having a little boy had made Daniel jealous. She wanted more than anything to keep him happy. At times she thought she would like a baby – after all, she had found she liked children now that she had got to know some. And she often thought of Marty. She fantasised about going back to see her family. She wanted to know how Marty was. Maybe Rose was finding things a struggle and she could help her. She even thought of sending money anonymously. She could not understand her fears about getting pregnant. Why did she feel this way? It must be because Daniel was so much older: their child would lose its father young, as she and Rose had.

She knew it had been hard for them both, and though Rose had never put it into words, she did not have to. It had made their relationship with their mother difficult. It was hard to lose a parent in any circumstances, but for a child to lose a parent could be much harder to come to terms with.

But she dared not say so to Daniel. How could she mention his own death to him?

And what if it's me overreacting, she said to herself. Why can't I just forget about it and live a normal life? So what if my baby loses its father young? He will have other family. Daniel will leave us loads of money. It may even bring me closer to Angela. She might forgive me.

She loved Daniel very much and yet somehow she could not do this for him and this made her feel very guilty. It was much too late now to tell him that she had been taking the Pill since before their marriage.

'Let's stay as we are for a bit longer, darling,' she said, trying to put a lightness in her voice she could not feel. 'I want you all to myself. And you may not love me when I'm fat.'

'That is nonsense,' said Daniel. 'You would be a perfect mother and you'd have perfect children. All women want children; it's a natural thing. You shouldn't be afraid of child-birth, my darling. It's a perfectly wonderful, natural thing.'

'What would Angela and Lauren think, Daniel?' she said. 'You're their dad, how would they feel if you have children younger than theirs?'

Daniel suddenly lost his temper. 'It's none of their goddammed business!' he said.

Mary went to see Dr Schaeffer alone. He was an old family friend, a good ten years older than Daniel. She was afraid that if she did not go immediately, Daniel would insist on coming with her. She was told there was nothing physically wrong with her. That it was just a matter of time. Dr Schaeffer would not start tests until they had been trying to conceive for at least a year. Then there were tests he could do. She should go home and stop worrying. At her request, he agreed to write to both herself and Daniel, giving this opinion. Mary went to the library to find a book on infertility.

If she was to have to go through tests she wanted to be prepared. Should she come off the Pill before anyone found

102

out about it? Would Dr Schaeffer know she was on the Pill if he ran some tests? It would be the easy way out, she told herself: come off the Pill and no one would ever know. She had used her maiden name, smiling to herself at the term, and gone to see a doctor not known to the Hansens or the Mercers. Surely no one could find out he had been prescribing Mary Palmer the Pill?

She could just stop taking it now and then if she still didn't get pregnant they could do as many tests as they liked. She wanted to and yet the fear persisted. She knew she would continue to take the Pill.

She sat in the coffee room of a restaurant, reading about ovulation and temperature-taking. She had three months before her year was up. Three months to decide what she was going to do. She sat drinking coffee, absorbed in her book. Idly looking up, she saw a middle-aged man walking towards the table and just for a moment she thought it was Hartley. He looked like him, shortish and tubby, absent-mindedly looking for a free table. She opened her mouth to call 'Hartley'. But it was not him. She remembered meeting Hartley in the coffee bar in Mayfair.

I'm still living a life of deceit, she said to herself sadly. Still lying to the folks back home.

Mary started to have the dream again. The same dream: the downcast girl submitting to the publicly good man. Her desperate attempt to stop the girl from going out of the door. Clothing her night after night with the warm cardigan from her own body, feeling the warmth; then the still corpse and the shadowy figures of her mother and Joyce.

She awoke sluggishly and heard deep breathing next to her. In the dawn light she saw the back of the head on the pillow, the thick white hair, that familiar smell of the night-shirt, the just-dried-on-the-washing-line smell. She reached out to him, only half awake. 'Daddy,' she said sleepily.

Her husband woke and turned towards her and smiled,

reaching to take her in his arms. He was always so gentle. She knew he loved her and she loved him, she wanted things to be right. As he kissed her and began taking off her nightdress she relaxed. She'd always liked men with white hair.

15

Janey brought the kids twice a week to see Mary when she thought Daniel would not be home. The children clearly adored her and Mary noticed that they were much less friendly to herself. She supposed it had something to do with Angela.

Janey let the kids do much as they liked as she and Mary played loud music, shouting above it. Janey was full of tales; about Barbara, the Mercers' cleaner, who was very nosy and always complaining to Angela about the state of her room. 'She's refused to clean my room, unless I give up smoking, like I'd do it for *her*,' she said, rolling her eyes in mock horror. 'As if I cared. I didn't want that nosy old bat sorting through my things, anyway, so that's a result.' She drew on her cigarette.

'Barbara was all right, she wouldn't look through your things,' said Mary. 'She was a bit fussy, but she was always helpful to me when Martha and Dan got out of hand.'

'Oh, she loved you, thought you were the bee's knees. It's me she thinks is a lazy slag.' Janey was laughing loudly and lighting another cigarette.

'I'm sure she doesn't think that,' said Mary, reddening at the word 'slag'.

'Mary why do you never have any booze?' Janey said. 'Good God girl, what were you before you came here, a nun?'

Mary did not want to start drinking again and she knew Daniel would be very angry if he knew Janey had been drinking while in charge of the children.

'Yeah, that's right,' said Mary, laughing. 'No drink and no sex before I met Daniel, that was me.'

Mary had seen Lauren's baby only once and she was aware that neither she nor Angela wanted any contact with her apart from the fortnightly family dinners. Janey adored the little boy. 'He's really cute,' she said. 'Makes me go all broody.'

'What about you Mary, not pregnant yet?' As Mary shook her head, Janey said, 'Well that'll please Madam.'

'What do you mean Janey?'

'Oh sorry, I shouldn't have said that. Look Mary, I shouldn't be saying this. It's something I overheard Angela say to Lauren when she was over with the brat.' She stopped and took a long drag on her cigarette. Mary waited; she had a feeling she knew what was coming. 'It's not that she doesn't like you, Mary, they both like you.' Janey stubbed out her cigarette and immediately lit another one. 'Jesus, I could use a drink,' she said. 'Mary, don't you drink at all?'

Mary just shook her head. She has decided she did not want to hear what Angela thought of her. And she certainly was not going to sit drinking with Janey. She did not dare.

'Well,' said Janey, 'Angela does like you. She just wishes you had gotten on that plane. That's what she said. OK, this is how it went. Lauren was showing off her baby. And Angela said: "What I dread is that the blessed virgin might get pregnant. How I wish she had gotten on that plane." This seemed to upset Lauren. But I didn't get to hear any more. They saw me and they both shut up.'

A noise from the bathroom sent them rushing to see what the kids were doing. They had climbed onto the bathroom chair and taken everything out of the cabinet. Martha was lavishly applying Mary's make-up to Dan's face. She had already slapped a generous amount on her own. Janey rushed in, chiding them good-naturedly.

'Come on, kids, you should ask Mary before you use her make-up,' she said. She picked up the scattered contents of the make-up bag including Mary's contraceptive pills. She put them all back in the bag and handed it to Mary. Mary knew she had seen the pills. She must know what they are, she thought, and yet she hasn't mentioned them. Mary wondered if she should say something and then decided against it. Probably Janey thought nothing of it. It wasn't unusual to be on the Pill, after all.

That evening Daniel came in looking troubled and angry. Mary knew something had been troubling him for days, but whatever it was he had not shared with her. 'What is it darling?' she said.

He poured himself a large whisky. He did not answer for a moment. Mary knew by now it was best not to ask questions but to let him tell her in his own time. Finally he said he had been with Angela. 'I knew something was wrong,' he said. 'She's been unhappy lately, and she wouldn't tell me why.'

'Oh I'm sorry about that Daniel,' said Mary. 'Is it something to do with the kids?'

'No, it's Michael,' said Daniel. 'Angela suspects . . . I hardly know how to say this, I cannot believe it of Michael. Of course I can believe it of that little whore.'

'What do you mean? You don't mean Janey?'

'She's not certain. She hasn't confronted that girl. Of course she would deny it.'

'But Michael wouldn't, surely, why does she suspect him?' said Mary.

'You know what that girl is like, always flirting with men. She tried it with me and I soon put her straight.' Mary smiled, for some reason this seemed funny. Daniel got angry. 'What is so amusing? Does it amuse you that my poor girl is going through this?'

'No of course not, Daniel. I just couldn't imagine Janey trying to flirt with you. You're not the flirty type darling. You're too straightforward.'

'Neither is Michael "the flirty type". It's that Janey. I don't want her here again.' I knew she was no good. And now she's putting my girl through hell.'

'But can you be sure Daniel? Have you asked Michael? Has Angela asked him? How could they be having an affair? They live under the same roof. Janey is always with the kids. I don't see how.'

'She goes out nights,' said Daniel. 'And so does Michael. Well, I've put a tail on that girl. We'll soon know what she does with her time off. But I tell you, she must not come here again.'

107

16

Mary was not looking forward to dinner with Angela and Michael. Martha and Dan had grown away from her and much preferred to be with Janey.

Angela was alone when Daniel and Mary arrived and there were no caterers in attendance. There was no sign of Lauren and Charles. The Mercers always had the services of a waitress and a butler but now Angela seemed to have taken charge. She looked tired and paler than usual; Mary noticed she wore no make-up. There was hardly any conversation at the table and Janey and the kids had not appeared at all.

Mary wondered if Janey was home. Daniel had said nothing to her about any results of the private detective he had following her. Maybe he changed his mind, she thought. It seemed a silly idea anyway. She knew Janey was a flirt and liked a good time, but Michael! He's too stuffy for Janey, she told herself. And he loves Angela. He would never do anything to hurt her or the kids.

Mary helped Angela to clear the table and load the dishwasher while Michael and Daniel sat with their brandy, not talking. Finally, Daniel said, 'I have something to say and I wish to God I did not. I would do anything not to have to say this.'

Angela sat down slowly at the table, then looked into Michael's face. Mary decided Angela knew what was coming. She wished she could leave the room. She felt sure Daniel had heard some news from his private detective. Mary did not want to hear it. Michael had been drinking more than usual. He sat expressionless, waiting. It seemed an age before Daniel spoke again.

'Michael,' he said, 'I trusted you, we all trusted you. I would never have suspected that you could do this. Just tell me why?'

Michael said nothing.

'I always suspected that girl,' continued Daniel. 'I had her tailed, Michael. You must know what I'm going to say. Why did you do it? How could you cheat on my daughter with a little slut like that?'

Angela got up suddenly and left the room. Mary stayed where she was; they had probably forgotten she was there.

'No one could ever measure up to you Daniel,' said Michael. 'Brilliant lawyer, wonderful father, perfect husband.' His voice was slurred with drink. 'What was the point of trying?'

'That little whore,' muttered Daniel.

'Don't blame Janey,' said Michael. 'Don't, just don't. She's been a lifeline to me. She made me laugh. She made me feel real. She wasn't always comparing me unfavourably to her wonderful dad. Don't blame Janey.'

'How dare you blame Angela! How dare you defend that slut in my daughter's house? I do, I blame her, and I'm going to tell her so.' He left the room.

Michael's speech was slurred. 'Yeah, Daniel,' he said. 'Your daughter's house, your ex-wife's money, your brilliant career.' He looked at Mary. 'So, angelic one, you've been holding out on us.'

'What do you mean?' said Mary, but she knew. She knew Janey had told him about the Pill.

Michael did not tell his wife immediately that Mary took the Pill. He waited until Angela asked him for a divorce.

17

Daniel decided Mary must see a shrink. A girl with a morbid fear of pregnancy must need psychiatric help. He found it very hard to forgive her for lying to him, for taking the Pill without consulting him. But he understood that she had natural fears. He reassured her: 'Just go and talk, Mary. It's all right for you to be worried about childbirth. Just go and see the shrink.'

Florence Webster was well into her sixties. She wore rather mannish clothes, long skirts and shapeless jackets in dull colours. She had short, grey hair and small spectacles. Mary thought she would be better suited to a monocle. She looked like something out of P.G. Wodehouse. Mary could find nothing sympathetic about her. She could not understand the reasons behind her questions. She seemed to Mary to be very cynical and unfeeling. Mary tried to answer her questions, which were all about her childhood and her feelings about her mother and father.

After six weekly sessions Mary felt confused and upset and Daniel had become silent and withdrawn. Though he resisted the idea at first, Daniel had finally agreed that she could stay on the Pill, at least until she made some progress with Florence Webster. She had pleaded with him that it was difficult enough trying to understand why she feared pregnancy without risking an actual conception before she had sorted herself out. He reluctantly agreed. But she suspected he secretly felt she was making a fuss about nothing. She did not feel the analysis was getting her anywhere and wanted to stop it.

At her seventh session Mary could do nothing but cry.

Florence Webster did not show her any sympathy. 'As a species we are still evolving, Mary,' she said. 'We are not as far away as you might think from our primate ancestors, perhaps "incestors" is a more accurate word. You knew your mother because she breast-fed you. A female on heat might mate with who-knew-what male in the tribe, commonly the most dominant. It would not be possible to pick out your father. The taboo is a comparatively recent phenomenon.'

'But what do you mean?' said Mary, thinking the women must have gone mad. 'You can't think that is all right now.'

'It's neither right nor wrong, Mary. It just is.'

'You have married a man who is old enough to be your father, and who acts *in loco parentis*, telling you that you should want a child: that it would be normal to want *his* child. Mary, does it feel normal to marry someone who behaves like an authoritarian father? Would it feel normal to have his child?'

'I can't believe that, I can't,' said Mary. 'Are you saying that this is the reason I am afraid of having children?'

'Some might say it is courageous,' Florence Webster went on. 'Some might just as easily say it is cowardly.' She paused and smiled at Mary. 'Or it's neither. It's just you, just what you think. That's all there is, Mary, that's it.'

Florence Webster was wearing her 'That's the end of the session' look, which meant Mary could not say anymore. Her time was up. She hated that. She could be crying hard or desperately needing to ask something but it was always the same. When her 55 minutes were up Florence Webster shut up shop immediately and became a waxwork image.

'Daniel I can't go back to her, I can't,' said Mary. She looked at her husband, willing him to be sympathetic. Willing him to smile at her like he used to and say it would be all right.

But Daniel was cold towards her. He said he was going to see Angela who was having a bad time owing to Michael's infidelity. 'She has *real* problems,' Mary. 'Yours are nothing compared to hers. You need to get grip on yourself. You are young. I have always been good to you and you want for

111

nothing, and yet you cannot behave like a proper wife. You continue to behave like a child.'

Mary did not want him to go. She was hurt and confused by what Florence Webster had said. One moment she thought it would be easier to just come off the Pill and get pregnant and the next she knew she could not.

'Please don't go yet, Daniel,' she said, putting her arms around him. She felt his body stiffen. The look on his face was cold and hard.

'Mary, I have to go and see my daughter,' he said. 'She needs me.'

As he left the apartment the telephone rang. It was Janey. 'I'm sorry Mary,' she said, 'I didn't mean to tell Mike about . . . you know . . . I mean, I didn't know it was a secret.'

Mary had to get out of the apartment; she was worried about Daniel's attitude. She was afraid. Why was he going now to see Angela? Had she found out about Hartley and the past? She said quickly, 'Janey let's meet, I need to talk to you.'

Janey was contrite. 'I didn't know, Mary,' she said. 'I was out with some mates in a bar. We bumped into Mike and some of his snooty lawyer friends. Nothing was supposed to happen. I didn't mean it to. We shared a cab home and he was a bit down. He never criticises Angela. But he was down. It just happened. We started to see each other. We were just talking. He said something about Angela not wanting you and Daniel to have children. And I said there was no chance of that because you were on the Pill. That was really it.'

But Mary was not really listening. The problem of the Pill was fast receding. She was worrying now about what Angela and Daniel were talking about.

'Mary, there's something else,' said Janey, and somehow Mary sensed what was coming. 'It was something Mike said. He was really angry with Daniel, he blames him for everything because compared to him no man is really good enough for Angela or Lauren. He said no matter how well he did at law he would never match up to Daniel Hansen.'

'What are you getting at?' said Mary. 'What do you mean "there's something else"?'

112

'It was Mike. He got very drunk the other night and he said – I'm sorry Mary – but he said "Daniel tells me not to sleep with whores. He should take his own advice. He's not the only one to do some private detective work. I know all about Mary's Geoffrey Hartley. I checked him out. Daniel's child bride is not all she seems." I asked him but he wouldn't say any more. Who is this Geoffrey Hartley, Mary?'

'He was someone I worked for in London. He gave me a reference when I got the job with the Mercers. Michael overheard me on the phone, talking to him. I can imagine what he thought. They are lawyers, aren't they? It would be easy to check someone out. I've had it now, mate.'

Her only thought was that she must call Hartley. She must have a contingency plan. Maybe Michael or Angela, or even – she felt dead inside at the thought – Daniel, may have spoken to him already.

'But why should he be such a problem?' asked Janey. 'So he gave you a glowing reference; he didn't actually lie, did he?'

'Yes, you could say that he lied,' said Mary.

'Tell me. What did he lie about? Didn't you work for him as a nanny, then?'

'No,' said Mary. 'Not as a nanny. Nothing like one, in fact. Look, please don't ask me. I can't talk about it now.'

'Well, I think that's mean,' said Janey. 'I've told you every-thing. I'll only think the worst, you know.'

'I expect if you ask Michael he will tell you, but I really don't want to talk about it,' said Mary.

'I doubt if I'll be seeing Mike again before I go home,' said Janey. 'Look Mary, I'm staying with Barbara.' Janey laughed at Mary's surprised look. 'Yeah, the old bag isn't so bad after all. She said I could stay with her until I go home. She's told me some interesting things about Angela.'

'I don't want to know,' said Mary. 'What kind of interesting things?'

'Well, Angela never had a nanny when her ma was alive. She did a lot more around the house. Barbara just used to help her out. But she's known the family for years. She worked for Angela's mother before.'

'What was she like?' asked Mary.

'Alicia? Well she had pots of money of her own for a start. She didn't have to marry stuffy old Daniel. Her dad was a lawyer too, and left her loads. Apparently she was a great help to Daniel in his career. Even though, according to old Barb, she really wanted to practice law herself.'

'But Daniel said he and the kids came first with her. He said she gave up the law when she married him. I thought it was because she wanted children.'

'Well, she didn't give it up without a fight, according to Barb. Mrs Hansen was not a happy woman in the end. She left Angela and Lauren all her money, too.' Janey was now warming to her story. 'Their apartments were paid for by her, and almost everything else. She didn't leave anything to Daniel. It was all willed to her daughters. Poor Mike, he never stood a chance. He couldn't compete with daddy's success or mummy's money. You can't blame him, really. But he still loves her, you know. He doesn't really want a divorce and he misses the kids.'

'You mean you still see him?' asked Mary.

'No, we're not "seeing" each other. It really was just a fling. No, he came round to see Barb. They're real mates, apparently, I didn't know that. Anyway, he wants Angela back. He's soft, is Mike. He isn't really the lawyer type. He's only doing it for Angela, and look where that's got him.'

Mary was dreading going back to the apartment. Would Daniel be there? And Angela? She was shaking as she put the key in the lock. Daniel was alone, waiting for her return.

'I'm not going to ask you where you've been,' he said. 'It matters to me not at all.'

She could do nothing but wait in silence for him to present the evidence for the prosecution. She was glad the courtroom was empty.

'You will leave this house,' he said. 'I have already begun

114

proceedings. There will be no settlement. We will fly you back from whence you came. I have nothing more to say.'

'Can I make one telephone call, please Daniel?' she said.

'Is that all you have to say, you despicable little whore? You deceived me from the word go. All the time you pretended to be an innocent you'd slept with all those men. You had worked as a prostitute in London. In order to fraudulently leave the country you passed yourself off as a decent innocent girl, looking after children. That is the worst part. That you could even think of spreading your corrupting influence to children. And to think that I wanted you to have *my* child, you, who are not fit—' He paused for breath. 'You are abhorrent to me Mary, I want you out of this apartment now.'

'Can I call home please, Daniel?'

'Home? What do you mean, your pimp? Yes, you may call him. Tell him your flight leaves in four hours.' You will take nothing with you. Your Geoffrey Hartley can collect you when you arrive in London. I'll get a taxi for you.' And he turned and left the room. He returned stony-faced to add: 'From this moment, you will not use my name.'

Mary dialled Hartley's number, praying he would be there. Hartley listened gravely while she told him what had happened.

'Don't cry, baby,' he said. 'I'll meet your plane. You can stay here. Don't worry about anything. Anton is looking forward to seeing you,' he added.

Daniel watched Mary pack the few belongings she was permitted to take with her, standing in the doorway of the bedroom regarding her with pure loathing. Mary was beyond tears. She looked at Daniel. She had got used to being with him. He had been kind and she had begun to feel very happy and comfortable. She loved him.

'I married you because you rescued me from being sent home. I liked and trusted you but that's all it was, then. But now I love you Daniel, believe me, I do. I can't have children. It frightens me to think why, but I can't. It frightened me what she said, what Florence Webster said about my Dad. She

115

seemed to think marrying you was something to do with my Dad. But I do love you Daniel, please believe that.'

'That is *lunacy*. What has that woman put into your head? Marrying me was nothing to do with your dad. We were husband and wife. We were intimate. Is this Webster woman suggesting something obscene about your father? That your relationship with your own father was not as it should have been? That you married me as a father substitute?' Daniel was white with anger.

'Please Daniel, please believe me . . .'

'Don't say any more,' he said. 'I wouldn't want be driven to strike you, despite what you've done. At least I can say I have never struck a woman.' He turned and walked away from her.

He had left some money for the taxi and her airline ticket on the hall table. When the taxi arrived he would not leave his study to say goodbye. It was finally over.

18

'What do you want? How did you get in here? I told the porters you were never to be allowed near my children again.' Angela was shaking with anger as she confronted Janey in the kitchen.

'Sorry, Angela I had to talk to you. Look I'm going back to England. I haven't seen Mike – Michael. It wasn't what you thought, anyway.'

'How dare you tell me what I thought,' said Angela. 'How did you get into my apartment?'

'I let her in,' said Barbara, appearing at the door. 'She's staying with me until she goes home. Just let the girl say what she has to say and then she'll go.'

At that moment little Dan appeared behind her and saw Janey. He rushed towards her.

'Please, Angela, I'm not trying to cause trouble, honestly I'm not. You knew what I was before. You knew I liked a laugh and had boyfriends. I didn't take you in.'

'Are you comparing that with sleeping with my husband?'

'He wasn't doing so well workwise and he didn't want to let you down. He couldn't talk to you so he talked to me, that's all. It wasn't planned and it only happened once. We were both drunk.' She stopped as she saw the disgust and pain on Angela's face. 'Look, I'm going back home. Mike never really wanted me. He wanted you and he still does. He told me so and he told Barb as well. Please don't divorce him.'

Angela sent Dan out of the room and asked Janey to leave. 'My father is arriving soon. He had better not find you here.'

'Please will you think about what I said,' said Janey. 'Mike loves you and the kids. I know he does.'

'Did he ask you to come and see me?'

'No, Angela, he doesn't know. I haven't seen him. But he doesn't want a divorce. And he wishes he hadn't told you about Mary being on the Pill. He thinks you and Mr Hansen were very hard on her. Please believe me.'

'Hard on her? A prostitute who deliberately and fraudulently passes herself off as a nanny when things got too hot for her in England? A seventeen-year-old girl whose own family had disowned her? *We* were hard on *her*?'

'But she was good with the kids and they loved her. She never went anywhere. She behaved more like a nun that anything. How was that being dishonest? I don't think she had any choice but to go on the game.'

'There is *always* a choice,' said Angela. 'I saw Mary in London; there was a man from somewhere in the building hanging around her. I should have realised. There was something about him and his behaviour. It was over-familiar and he had a very insinuating manner. And Mary looked ashamed. It thought it was odd, I should have listened to my instinct, but unfortunately I did not. And look what has happened. I allowed my own father to be taken in by a lying, common little whore.

'I wondered why she never called her family. Now it seems they threw her out, too, That little tart lied to us all. How do I know that she and Michael . . .' Here she broke off, sobbing, and Janey went to put her arms around her.

'Janey, what am I going to do? I know, I know Mary did behave like a nun, and you *are* right, I do want him back. But how can I? How can I?' She drew a deep breath and tried to compose herself. 'Look, you must go now. Dad is coming soon and he mustn't find you here, Janey. You must go.'

Daniel Hansen had come to tell Angela that his divorce from Mary was soon to be finalised. He would be free of her. 'I expected her to at least fight for some sort of settlement, but I haven't heard from her.'

118

'But you'll be rid of her soon, Dad, she'll be just a bad memory. And then she'll be gone.'

Daniel sat silently for some minutes. 'A bad memory,' he repeated. 'Except, you know now that it's over, I can't remember anything bad about her. When I first met her I thought she was so sweet. Of course she was a whore and she hid that from us. But she never protested, Angela. I said some terrible things to that girl. I really thought she would retaliate. I expected to see her in her true colours. But she just said she had grown to love me.'

'How can you believe that? She just didn't want to go back to her family. They threw her out as well. She'll just go back to this Hartley and continue as she did before. They all lie. I just had Janey here, telling me that Michael still loves me. But how could he? How could he do what he did and still love me?'

'What did that girl say, has she been in touch with Mary?' asked Daniel.

'No, no, Dad, she didn't mention Mary, she just said I should take Michael back. She said that he turned to her because he couldn't talk to me about doing badly at work. As if I'm unapproachable. As if he couldn't come to me.'

'There was something Mary said,' said Daniel. 'About her psychoanalysis. She was very upset and confused about it. I think I'll go and see this Mrs Webster.'

'But what good would that do, Dad? You know shrinks never divulge what has been discussed with their clients.'

'I am just trying to understand, Mrs Webster, why she became a prostitute. Did she simply let a middle-aged man manipulate her like that? Get her to sleep with all those men? But why did she go through with it? When everything that is decent should have told her it was wrong'

'What was it about her, then, that you wanted – you being a middle-aged man?

Daniel looked annoyed. Then he got angry. 'Wanted from

119

her? I wanted nothing from her but that she be a proper wife. We are not here to talk about me, Mrs Webster.'

Mrs Webster did not blink. 'Are we not?' she said. 'Do you not think we could throw some light on what went wrong with your marriage? Is that not why we are here?'

'No, no. There was nothing wrong with our marriage that we could not have fixed. What I am trying to understand is what led her to the life she had in London. She could have been anything she wanted. She's pretty and smart. She just lacks confidence in herself. She's afraid of people. She never wanted to go out and meet people. She was happy just to be with me. But she knew I loved her and yet she lied to me about the Pill. Why?'

'Why do you think she lied?'

'She was a gold-digger, she wanted to trap me. She had no intention of being a proper wife,' said Daniel.

'And what was your intention?'

'Why do you keep bringing this back to me Mrs Webster? I've told you this is not about me? It's about a seventeen-year-old prostitute who sees her chance to become respectable.'

'By becoming a nanny?'

'Yes, and by seizing the chance of becoming the wife of a respectable man.'

'And what was your intention, Mr Hansen?'

'I wanted her. I wanted us to be a proper family. To have children and a proper life together.'

'And she pretended she was willing, before you married her, to have children?'

'Of course, all women want children.'

'But this is a seventeen-year-old and you are fifty-one.'

'What did she say to you? What did she say about me?'

'In my professional work with a client I merely hold up a mirror, Mr Hansen. She was a very troubled girl. And if I may say so you are a very troubled man, otherwise you would not have come to me.'

'I came to you to find out about her, and you keep talking about me. I'm going to end this interview, Mrs Webster.'

'Might I suggest that you have come to me to find out

120

about yourself, Mr Hansen? If you wish to know about your wife, you must talk to her.'

'She didn't understand herself, how could she explain herself to me?'

'But you lived with her as man and wife for – how long was it? A year? What conclusion did you reach?

'I could never have believed she was a whore. She thoroughly deceived me.'

'Do you think she married you merely to be respectable?'

'She saw her chance, she had left my daughter's employ and was about to be sent home. Becoming my wife was her only chance. Her only chance of a decent life. She had no money and nowhere to go except back to her pimp. Yes, I see, I was just about preferable to her pimp.'

'She asked you to intervene to stop her being sent home?'

'No, no, but she must have known I wouldn't let her go.'

Mrs Webster sat motionless and said nothing.

'So what do you have to say to that? She married me so she wouldn't have to return to an uncertain future.'

'What do you say to it, Mr Hansen? What do you say about this choice made by, to paraphrase you, an "easily-led teenager"?'

'So I'm the bad guy here, is that what you're saying? I'm the bad guy for loving her, for taking her in, for expecting her to have my kids?'

'If you knew more about her childhood, her experiences in London, perhaps you might be able to answer that question for yourself,' said Mrs Webster. 'And now, Mr Hansen, this session is at an end.'

121

19

By the time Mary arrived in London she had lost track of time. She did not know what day it was. Hartley was waiting for her, looking thinner than she remembered him, and bleary-eyed from lack of sleep.

'Do you know it's four a.m.?' he said, laughing and hugging her. 'I've been waiting for you all night.' Mary clung to him, sobbing like a child. 'Come on, baby,' he said. 'Come home and tell me all about it.'

When they got home Anton was making breakfast. He smiled at Mary and looked pleased to see her. As Mary told her story she observed the unlikely couple, one a tall, lean, 30-year-old American, the other a short, balding, slightly less chubby than she remembered him 58-year-old, sitting opposite her drinking tea.

Hartley had been complaining about having to eat cereal and fruit. 'I was brought up on eggs and bacon,' he said. 'It's too late now to get me to eat this stuff.'

'Come on Pop, and stop complaining,' said Anton. 'I have to look after your heart.'

'You already look after my heart,' said Hartley.

They both looked very tired, but Mary could see a change in them. They were more openly affectionate with each other and smiled a lot. They said the antiques business suited them very well. They had two people to look after the shop, both of whom had been with the former owner for more than 40 years.

'The shop practically runs itself,' said Anton. 'We spend our time merrily driving around the country, buying from auctions and sales.'

They said Mary was lucky to catch them as they were often out of London and lived for most of the time in Hartley's old family house in Norfolk.

'Norfolk is a great base for our game,' said Anton, smiling. Mary could never remember him smiling so much. Living in Norfolk meant they could also keep an eye on Mrs Hartley who was now getting old and frail. They were very happy with their lot, they said, laughing at their silly auctioneers' joke.

'We have no time for the old game now,' said Hartley. 'So you'll be safe with us, little girl.' Again they both laughed and Mary asked them what had happened to them.

'You both used to be, well, more cautious,' she said.

'We're contented, that's all,' said Anton. 'Believe me, there is no substitute for it.'

Mary felt a pang of jealousy. And she felt hurt that they appeared to dismiss her awful experience in New York as just another job that didn't work out. 'I was married to Daniel, you know,' she said petulantly. 'Still am, until the divorce is final. We were happy. If I could have had a baby we would still be happy.'

'You said you couldn't let yourself get pregnant. Why was that?' asked Anton.

'I don't know, I just don't know.' Mary suddenly felt sadder than ever.

'But you're still a kid. You're just too young, that's all. And how old is your husband?'

'He's fifty-one.'

'Well,' said Hartley, 'there you are then. You need someone nearer your own age if you're going to have children.'

'Oh, so it was all right to make me fuck all those fifty-year-olds then!' shouted Mary. She was suddenly really angry. 'That was *fine*. Just don't go marrying one of them. Oh no, that's not *normal*.' They smiled at her indulgently which made her angrier still. 'I *miss* him,' she said. 'We were happily married.' They stopped smiling but still to her mind were not taking her plight seriously enough.

'It couldn't have been as bad as being a whore,' joked Anton. 'Surely there is a huge difference between being a child bride and being a whore? Less tiring. Maybe fewer surprises.'

The joke seemed such a cruel one to Mary that she looked at Anton in astonishment. Then she suddenly thought of Simon. He was always laughing at her, too. She remembered him saying that she was someone who took herself too seriously. She decided to give Anton the benefit of the doubt, and laughed, too.

They were about to sell the flat in Mount Street, but said that Mary could stay there until the sale was completed. But Mary did not want to. She felt a bit piqued that they could be so insensitive to her feelings to think she could live there after what had happened to her.

'Look, Mary I have to get some sleep,' said Hartley. 'Why don't you think about learning the antiques trade? I'm sure we have an opening for a junior in the shop.'

Mary found this very funny. 'Great idea Hartley,' she said 'I've become adept at handling antiques.'

'Good God,' said Anton. 'Uptight little Mary has made a joke. Is this the first ever?'

'Don't worry,' said Hartley. 'We'll get you a little flat somewhere nice. With nice neighbours and good security You can work in the shop, Barry and Norman will look after you. They're another happy couple.'

'We'll pay you a pittance and give you the flat as part of your pay,' said Anton, laughing again.

20

'When she left she did not reproach me. She said she had married me because I was kind to her and she did not want to go back to England. But she had grown to love me. And I know that is true. She loved me. She did love me. Nothing else matters. I know it now. She loved me. I never took into account what she had been through, losing her dad so young, living in a house with no love or affection. Not being able to mix well with people. Of course she was a prey for the unscrupulous. And what did I do? Tried to make her have my children. She was scarcely more than a child herself.'

'You say she loved you, Dad, but what about in ten years, or twenty? When you would be seventy and she would be only thirty-nine? What then? She'd bound to leave you then,' said Angela. 'What then?'

'I'd have had twenty years of loving that sweet and beautiful girl. I'd have had the best twenty years of my life. Why did you do it, Angela? Why did you have Michael check up on that Hartley guy? If you hadn't I would never have known. Mary would have gotten over this silly fear of childbirth. It was probably due to all the awful experiences she'd had. And even if she couldn't have children, it wouldn't matter. I can see that now. I'm remembering her, I can't stop thinking and remembering how sweet she was. And she never had a bad word to say about anyone.'

'She was just two-faced, Dad,' said Angela, but her father ignored her.

'If I could just have her back. I would move heaven and earth to have that sweet girl back.' He sat silently staring out of the window. Then he turned to look at Angela. 'Take him

125

back, my dear. Michael, I mean. He still loves you and I know you still love him. Don't be a fool like your old dad. What he did was foolish but I dare say he thought he had his reasons. You were upset about me marrying so soon after your mother. And I'm not an easy act to follow,' he added, trying to laugh. 'Take him back Angie.'

'I can't Dad. I'm going through with the divorce. I want to start again.'

No you don't, baby. I know my girl. You want Michael back and all you have to do is ask him. And the kids miss him. They want their dad. They need their dad.'

'They can still see Michael. I won't stop them from seeing him. But I won't take him back. He's humiliated me.'

'We humiliated *him*, Angela. I am afraid to say that we did. I don't blame him if he never forgives me. Your mother was right.'

'Right about what? What do you mean?'

'She could see, she could see how Michael felt. She wouldn't talk to you about it. But she thought I was hard on him. Alicia thought I was hard on everyone, except you, my angel. You have always been the apple of my eye. I never felt that Michael was good enough. I never gave him a chance. Take him back, Angela.'

'It's too late Dad, I'm afraid it's too late.'

'No, it is not. And it's not too late for me, either. I'm going to find out where Mary is. I've already begun. It shouldn't be hard to find her.'

'Dad, don't. Where's your pride? People will laugh if you go running after that little whore. Dad, listen to me. Mary went straight back to this, this Hartley, and straight back on the game. What else is she fit for?'

Daniel continued as if she had not spoken. 'We'll live in London. I've always loved the place. Or if not London some other city. There are many fine cities in England. I'm determined Angela. I want her back.'

21

Mary found Barry and Norman easy to be with. They were a homosexual couple in their early sixties, whose entire working life had been spent in the little Mayfair antiques shop. Under their guidance she began to learn about the history of the furniture and works of art which crowded the shop floor and the large gallery beneath. They had lived above the shop since the death of the owner 18 months before and were dedicated to the work and devoted to each other. They encouraged Mary to go to classes to learn the finer points of the trade and told Hartley that she was an excellent pupil with a real feel for old things. When Hartley repeated this to Mary he was laughing. 'It's just what you always said baby, this is what your two professions have in common.'

It was Norman who told Mary that a very handsome American gentleman had been asking for her. He had left his card. Even before she saw it Mary knew it would read: Daniel Hansen, Attorney at Law.

'What did he say?' she asked Norman anxiously. 'Did he seem angry?'

'Well, no, he wasn't angry. A bit stern, perhaps. But if you don't want to see him, then don't.' He laughed at her. Mary felt hurt. Yet another person was laughing at her. She had studied her face many times in the mirror, wondering what people found funny about it.

'Why are you laughing, Norman?' she asked him.

'Well, I suppose the funniest thing about you, Mary, is that you take yourself so seriously,' was his reply. 'You're only nineteen or twenty aren't you? But when do you ever go out and have fun? I have never seen you laugh at all.'

'And that makes me funny?' said Mary. And he just laughed in reply.

'Oh, and Mary,' said Norman. 'Hartley said to tell you that Simon is in London and to ask if you would like to see him. He said he would understand if you did not, so don't be afraid to say.'

Mary decided impulsively to see Simon and not Daniel. She had taken in what Norman had said to her. He was right when he said she never had any fun. She had never really been able to make friends. Even at school she had felt isolated from her classmates. Unless Simon had come to London with Mireille, he might take her out somewhere. Then she could stop herself thinking about Daniel.

She called Hartley and said if Simon was in London alone then she would see him. Simon arrived in the shop within 20 minutes of her call to Hartley.

'You look wonderful, Mary,' he said. 'More beautiful than ever.'

'Simon,' she said, 'do you know about my marriage?'

He nodded, saying that Hartley had told him, sparing him no gruesome detail.

'Look, Simon, I've never asked you for anything have I? But I need a favour.'

Simon folded his arms and regarded her with mock gravity. 'Well, go on then, ask away,' he said as she hesitated.

'Daniel is here, in London, and I don't want to see him. Could we go somewhere, for the weekend or something? Somewhere a fairly long away. He might come back and I don't want to bump into him. If I'm not here he'll go back to New York. I know it's silly of me.'

Simon was smiling. 'And you call that a favour? You ask me take you away for a weekend and you think I'm doing you a favour?'

'I don't know what you mean.'

'Well, what about ten days in Italy? I have to go to Rome. I'm working there on a film from tomorrow. Come with me, Mary, you really would be doing me a favour.' He was laughing at her serious face. 'After all it's not as if there would be

128

ny gorgeous girls around, so you really would be helping me
out.' As she still regarded him uncomprehendingly he
laughed louder. 'Mary I would love to take you away for a few
days,' he said finally. 'I had often dwelt at great length on one
of my favourite fantasies; spending time making love to you.
I've heard so many good things about your skills. Please say
something.'

Mary did not enjoy the thought of being the 'other woman'.
That Mireille was far away in California made it only slightly
more bearable. 'I will never forgive you for getting me on the
game. Whatever you say will not make that all right,' she said.
'No matter if you say it could have been worse. If you hadn't
rejected me my life would have been very different.'

Simon just laughed. 'Yes my darling, you would have gone
on working in an office, if you'd found another job that is, as
I recall it wasn't exactly your forte, until you finally turned
into your mother and died.'

'That's rubbish Simon. Look, I'll prove it to you. When we
get back from Italy I'm going to see my family. My Mum is
not as one-dimensional as you say. And I'm in a position to
help them out now, if they need it. At least they won't sneer
at me for being on the game. I have a proper job and my own
money now, and I don't have to pretend to anyone where it
came from.' She smiled suddenly at the thought of seeing
Marty again. 'Simon this is a one-off, or should I say ten days-
off. Don't imagine I am going to be here for you whenever
you are in London while you stay married to Mireille.'

'You're a born "other woman" Mary,' said Simon. 'Why
fight it?'

'I wasn't a "born" anything,' she protested.

'Okay, but you've never "bought" the family life bit. You
played at it. You like kids but only when you can give them
back. You never wanted to do the housewife bit.'

'But I did do the housewife bit, with Daniel, and it was one
of the happiest times of my life. I took cookery lessons. I
cooked everything Daniel liked. We had someone to clean
and do the ironing but I used to cook. We were happy. It was
a fairy tale, of course, but we were happy, for a while.

129

Unfortunately we were not living in the same fairy tale, so we couldn't share the same happy ending. I wanted to be secure. That's why I married him. He offered me security and no worries. I didn't realise I had married my Dad. Of course I couldn't have his kids. I couldn't have kids with my Dad, that was all.'

'Mary, that's just psychoanalytical mumbo jumbo. You married an older man, but you didn't marry your dad. That's nonsense.'

'But it's true, Simon. I didn't realise it at the time; it's the same thing. I didn't even realise it when he made me see the shrink. Though of course *she* knew. I thought the woman was crazy. I couldn't understand what she was getting at. She asked me loads of questions about my Mum and Dad and came to off-the-wall conclusions, as far as I was concerned. was totally confused and upset by what she said.'

'And all the time it was me you pined for,' laughed Simon, making his familiar mock bow.

Mary laughed at him. 'Simon, I had all but forgotten you by then, though oddly enough sometimes Daniel used to remind me of you. When he teased me, it used to remind me of you. And I remembered what you said. What was it? That some people laugh because they . . . what was it you said, I can't remember it exactly, but you meant I shouldn't have taken offence. You laughed at me because you thought I was sweet, or something like that. I realised then that Daniel teased me because he loved me too. Fortunately for you you're safely married to Mireille. And you know nothing will change that.'

'But I *love* you, Mary. Mireille is just a tidied up and controlled version of you. I prefer the screwed-up original. I'm always going to love you, Mary.'

'Yeah, and you're always going to be married to Mireille,' she said.

'She wouldn't live with me without marriage. I was so in love with her. I had to have her.'

'Was?' said Mary.

'Okay, am. I do love her still. But she would not live with

130

me without marriage. She was so beautiful and you never could tell what she was thinking. It was so sexy. She made a couple of films, and she was good in them. But more as a presence than an actress, bless her. She couldn't go on being a presence with no real acting ability to back it up.'

'She didn't do so badly,' said Mary.

'Don't be jealous my darling. You have no need to be jealous of Mireille. I love you Mary, you know that. But she would never divorce me. She's a good Catholic.'

'But you haven't got any children.'

'Okay, not that good a Catholic. But I didn't want to have children at all. She wouldn't live with me without marriage and then said she didn't feel it was right to be in a marriage without children. I had give way in the end. But of course her career had faltered by then, anyway. So her pregnancy has come in very handy for her.'

'She's pregnant! Why didn't you tell me?'

'Mary, I just have,' said Simon laughing. 'Oh come, on don't look so shocked. She's very happy about it.'

'*She's* very happy! And of course you'll stay together. In California you're the perfect couple. And soon you'll be the perfect family. And that is how you want it. You don't love me, Simon. We just go back a long way,' she said, laughing.

'Yes, my child, a long way, all of two years.'

'That's a long time to someone of my age, Mr Pushing Thirty.'

'So now you have everything you want and maybe a fat divorce settlement to come?'

'No chance. Daniel will see to that. But I do have everything I want now, thanks to Hartley. He was the first person who listened to me, do you know that? You didn't, Simon, my family didn't. He listened to me that day I couldn't go on being a tart, even though it meant a financial loss to him. And he hated having to find someone new, poor Hartley. You could've done better for him there, Simon, with the training of the new recruits, I mean.'

'I told you, Hartley's business wasn't in my mind, then. I just thought you were a silly little girl who would get pregnant

131

or fall in love with me. It got so boring, girls falling in love with me. Suddenly it just didn't seem worth the mess. I only told Hartley about you later because you looked so much in danger, hanging about the West End. Looking the way you did, so open and so vulnerable and so fucking sexy. And so lost. Believe me, you were in real danger. I had to tell Hartley about you.'

'Simon, you think I love you, but the only person, the only person I have ever loved, totally loved, is my father. Everything I have done is for him or because of him, everything. When you go back to the States I will miss you for a while. You're exciting to be with, but I won't really care. And I don't envy Mireille, being pregnant by a husband she'll never be able to trust.'

'Hey, come on, Mary, French women are much more sensible about these things,' protested Simon.

'You can still be hurt, even when you're being sensible,' said Mary. 'And you know it, Simon, you know it but you just don't care. With my Dad's death something died in me too. I sort of went numb. Oh, I know I looked for him, I looked for him in every man, however perverse or unlikely that may seem. In you, in Hartley in a bizarre way, and of course in Daniel. I looked for him; I searched for my lost love, my father. He's the only person I've ever loved.'

'That's obscene,' said Simon. 'It's positively pornographic. You don't know what you're saying. And anyway it's only because he died when you were so young and still needed him. If he'd died when you'd grown up it would have been different.'

'Of course, I know that,' said Mary impatiently. 'But he didn't die when I was grown up, he died when I was nine. I didn't realise it at first, of course, but what Hartley has done for me, taking me in and looking after me, has made him a sort of father in a funny way.'

Simon protested here: 'Mary, don't. He's a homosexual and a pimp, what are you saying?'

She ignored him. 'He bailed me out over and over. What would I have done if he hadn't taken me in after I got the

132

sack from the agency, or after Daniel? He gave me a job and a home even though I had walked out on him. My family never did that for me. I will repay him. He will always be able to count on me. I will do for Hartley what I didn't get the chance to do for my father.'

'You're talking pure rubbish. For God's sake you're only a kid. What you need is ten nights of passion with me. I may be pushing thirty but I'm the youngest man you've had by more than twenty years. Make the most of me.'

22

The day after her return from Rome the encounter she was dreading arrived, she heard someone enter the shop and looked up to see Daniel.

'How long will you be in London?' she asked him after the embarrassment of their greeting.

'Until we forget the past and until you want to be with me again,' he said. But his tone was flat and his face showed no enthusiasm for the idea. She knew that if it had not been for her fling with Simon she would not have had the courage to resist going back to him. A part of her wanted to. The part that still loved him. But she knew she would always be like a child to him; someone to be guided and told what to do. Someone who lived on what he decided was a fitting allowance; who never seriously questioned or disagreed with him.

Also, she felt she owed Hartley. He was not the same man. At first his weight loss suited him but it seemed to have accelerated and he sometimes complained of a lack of energy. Anton was worried, too, especially as he had to go to the States on business. He had made Mary promise to look after Hartley.

She looked at Daniel and could not understand why he wanted her. Was he afraid of getting old? 'Would having a young wife and children make you feel young, Daniel, is that it?'

'Mary, I have put an end to the divorce. I was too hasty with you and I regret the things I said. I want to understand why you did what you did.'

'Daniel, I don't want to hurt your feelings. How can I say this? I had an old Dad. And I lost him. Maybe if I had been a different kind of person I would have got over it. But it felt as if he went away, as if he left me. It may go deeper than that. I don't want to have a child. That is all I know. I can't have a child.'

'But we could at least talk about it, couldn't we? I could be in London for as long as it takes.'

'You will always be an authority figure to me now, Daniel,' she said. 'I can't help it. You didn't give me a chance to explain. Can't you see, much as I care for you it would never have been like a proper marriage. It's almost like you were a replacement for my Dad, you looked after me, and I did what you said.'

Daniel shook his head. 'You're talking nonsense,' he said. 'I'll be at my hotel if you change your mind.'

She had meant to ask after Angela and the children but had left it too late. Daniel had gone. She looked at his card – he had actually had a card printed with his London hotel number. She looked at it steadily. Then she tore it in two and put in slowly in the bin.

Anton was in LA visiting his father. He had not called for a couple of days and Hartley was worried. 'He calls me every day, and last time we spoke he was not well,' he said. 'I've called and called and got no answer.'

Finally they heard from a friend that Anton was in hospital. He had become ill and was getting weaker. They were trying various tests and were hopeful that they would discover what was wrong with him. Hartley decided he must go to be with him. When he telephoned Mary a few days later he was very upset.

'They think he has pneumonia,' he said. 'I'm worried about him. He's so thin and has no energy. I must stay with him.'

'Have you got your heart tablets?' said Mary anxiously. He ignored her. 'And don't eat all the wrong things, please Hartley.'

But she knew he was not listening. He was worried about Anton. And Mary worried that Anton's illness would make

135

Hartley ill. She could not contemplate what would happen if he got ill.

During Hartley's absence Mary became more involved with the business, taking over more duties from the ageing Barry and Norman. Without Hartley and Simon she felt very lonely. What had she hoped would happen with Simon? That he would leave Mireille? But even someone like Simon would not leave his wife while she was pregnant. And, thought Mary bitterly, even if he did leave her how could I ever trust him? Simon would always have affairs. And she realised as Mireille got older, even if he stayed with her, the affairs would not stop. That was just the way Simon was. He was the sexiest, most fascinating man she had ever known. And, she realised, he was a younger version of Daniel. The blond mane was now a head of thick white hair, but the self-assurance, the automatic assumption that he should do what he liked and have what he wanted was the same. Mary felt depressed. She knew she was too insecure to let herself love the younger man because opportunities for infidelity were constantly available to him.

Why am I so pathetic? she chided herself. Why do I need someone to be faithful to me anyway? The whole thing is a nonsense. She knew that Simon was not a good bet and she despised herself for needing someone. She concluded that young women reassure men whilst older men reassure women and that was that – she could see no way around it.

She wanted to call Daniel in New York but did not allow herself to, feeling she must be there for Hartley. With Anton so ill with pneumonia he needed her and she owed him. Barry and Norman were increasingly relying on her and there was no one to go to auctions. She was worried about the business but could not add to the pressure on Hartley.

Hartley called her whenever he could. He told her that Anton was very ill indeed. She called Simon who agreed things were serious.

'It's wearing poor old Hartley out,' he said. 'He looks dreadfully ill.'

Simon promised to keep Mary informed. Hartley always

made light of his own feelings. He stayed at Anton's bedside until he died, 'from a respiratory infection exacerbated by the weakened state brought on by pneumonia'.

When Hartley returned Mary could see that he was changed by the loss of his beloved Anton. He took very little interest in the business and suggested that Mary employ someone to go to auctions and do the buying so that she could concentrate on helping Barry and Norman to run the shop. Mary was saddened to see the change in him. He no longer wanted to go to Norfolk where he had been so happy with his lover.

Mary constantly worried and fussed over Hartley. But apart from his grieving, he said he was well. 'I'm getting old, baby,' he said to her. 'But you mustn't worry about me. You must go out and meet people of your own age and enjoy yourself. I'll be all right. Barry and Norman will look out for me.'

'But Barry and Norman are older than you Hartley,' she replied. But Hartley just smiled. Then his mother died suddenly and he just seemed to sink deeper. The house in Norfolk had been left to him and he decided to sell it. He did not have the heart to go there again.

Mary's loneliness and depression increased. She had made no friends. She had never, she realised, had friends. Barry and Norman increasingly depended on her while Hartley became sadder and more distant. Estate agents were calling about the sale of the house in Norfolk and Mary could not cope.

She wanted a drink but she feared it would get out of control. She needed to speak to someone. It was days before she realised she needed to speak to her husband. She assumed he was still her husband as she had heard no word of a divorce. It would be lunchtime in New York. Would he be at the office? Or having lunch somewhere? Maybe he was seeing someone else. Or several others. He was so good-looking and a catch. She decided not to call him. He would despise her for being so weak. She could not forget the look on his face as he watched her pack. She could not call him. She needed a drink.

The phone was ringing. It seemed to be coming from a long way away. She roused herself with difficulty. Her head hurt as she raised it from the cushion. She had been asleep on the settee. It was eight in the evening. She picked up the phone. It was Norman. 'Mary, are you all right? We haven't seen you in the shop since lunchtime. Hartley has been trying to get you. Are you all right?'

'Oh, don't worry, I had a headache, I'll call him. Thanks, Norman,' she said. But instead of calling him she went to see him. He looked at her quizzically.

'You're drinking again,' he said. 'I'm sorry baby, I know I drove you to it.'

Despite her thumping head she cooked him a meal and put him to bed. She knew then that Hartley was ill. She sat with him all night. He seemed delirious. He drifted in and out of sleep. By midnight he seemed settled and she made herself some tea, swearing that she would never drink again. She thought again of Daniel.

I must think of an excuse to call him, she told herself. She rejected asking after Angela and the kids. She rejected an update on the divorce situation. Finally she just dialled his number.

'Daniel? It's Mary.'

There was a long pause. 'Oh, Mary, hello,' he said. 'How are you?'

She had meant to say she was fine, she just wondered how he was and how the children were, how Angela was, how New York was, anything but what she actually said. 'Daniel everything is going wrong. Hartley is ill. Barry and Norman are getting too old to run the business, I have estate agents calling me every day about the property in Norfolk and I can't cope.'

'I'm still your husband, I'm still responsible for you,' he said stuffily.

'Why are you still my husband? What happened to the divorce?' she said sarcastically. But it was too much to expect that he would soften. She wished she had not spoken about divorce. But she despised herself. Why was she unable to say what she felt? 'I still feel you are way above me, Mr Hansen,' she said.

'If you need my help. I will give it,' he replied. 'I'll come to

London. I know where to find you.' In the silence that followed he hung up.

The phone immediately rang and Mary picked it up, thinking that it was Daniel calling back.

'Mary? Hi, it's me, Janey.'

'Janey, where are you?'

'I'm at home but I'm coming to London tomorrow. And I've got loads to tell you. Where can I meet you?' Then, before Mary could reply she screeched, 'I'm getting married! Isn't that great? Just wait till you see him.'

Janey arrived in the shop with a tall good-looking boy and introduced him to Mary as her fiancé. 'This is Mick, isn't he the most gorgeous hunk you ever saw?'

'Don't listen to the silly tart, Mary,' said Mick. 'She's daft.' Then he smiled straight at her and said, 'I've heard all about you, something about marrying a rich old geezer and then walking out on him?' He looked around the shop. 'Well he seems to have made it worth your while.'

'Don't worry darling, as soon as you're a millionaire, I'll do the same,' laughed Janey.

They were so outrageous Mary could only laugh. 'If you stick around you might meet the rich old geezer himself,' she said. 'His plane is due to land in an hour. That only gives us a couple of hours to gossip about him.'

'Well I'll be quick, then,' said Janey. 'I don't think Daniel would be pleased to see me. Let's get to the pub.'

Mary became wary. She did not want Daniel to find her in a pub. 'No. My favourite restaurant is just around the corner. I'll get us a table. Barry, I'll be about an hour and a half. Please tell Mr Hansen, if he arrives, when I'll will be back.'

'Why is Daniel coming to see you?' asked Janey. The last time I talked to Barbara he was divorcing you.'

'Come on Janey, let's go and eat. It's a long story. So it was Barbara. I was wondering how you got my number.'

In the restaurant Mary was careful not to drink any alcohol. For Daniel to find out that she drank too much would spoil everything. 'It's no good, Janey,' she said. 'I've tried not to, but I want him back.'

'But he was horrible to you,' said Janey. 'Are you mad? Let him divorce you and take the money.'

'It's no good, Janey, I can't cope on my own. Hartley is not at all well and anyway he's even older than Daniel. I have to stay with him. But I need Daniel. And I still love him. I don't really remember how it happened. But I do love him.'

'Who is Hartley?' asked Mick.

'He was my pimp,' replied Mary.

'You what?'

Janey guffawed. 'Well, Mary, you've changed. You used to be so prim. I thought you were two centuries after your time.' She turned to Mick. 'When I met this one here, she was a blushing bride, said she had never been out with boys, didn't drink, said she hadn't slept with her husband-to-be, and was wearing a wedding outfit even my granny would give to Oxfam.'

Mick leaned forward and grinned in Mary's face.

'Then I find she's on the Pill but her husband doesn't know, and then I find that before she was a nanny she was on the game. And now she's running an antiques business with her pimp and she wants her husband back. And all the while she looks like a girl guide.'

'Well,' said Mick, 'and why not? This rich old geezer could do a lot worse. At least he's getting a woman with experience.'

The three of them fell about laughing.

'Well, at least you know you're getting a virgin,' said Janey. 'Come on Mary, at least have a glass of wine.'

'Well, that's another thing,' said Mary. 'I have a tendency to drink too much sometimes. The other day I just lost about six hours and didn't hear the phone, or anything. I think it's time to go on the wagon.'

'Jeeesus,' said Janey. 'The next thing you'll be telling me is you're a bank robber. You must be like that bloke in the book, what was his name? Mick, you know the one I mean, he does all these wicked thing but he still has the face of an angel because all the bad shows on his portrait and not on his face.'

'Oh yeah,' said Mick. 'I know the one you mean, we read it

140

at school. So Mary, you're really forty-five and if I saw the picture in your attic I'd run away screaming?'

'Something like that,' said Mary. Her happy mood was evaporating. She was very nervous about seeing Daniel again. All I have to offer him is problems, she thought. She watched Janey and Mick happily teasing each other. They touched each other constantly, brushing shoulders, holding hands, kissing and play-fighting. They couldn't keep their hands off each other. Mary felt jealous. Perhaps I just need someone around. Perhaps I don't love Daniel at all. Perhaps that is all there is, just need, she thought.

'So, Mary, my gossip is old now. The last time I spoke to Barbara she said Daniel was divorcing you,' said Janey. 'I was coming to wish you well out of it.'

'How is Angela?'

'Oh, it's very sad. She's still refusing to see Mike – er – Michael. Martha and Dan see him but Angela won't. They're divorced now. But Barbara says she's very unhappy. And she says that Daniel blames himself for everything.'

'Not everything, surely.'

'Yep, even you, Mary. Apparently he keeps telling Angela she should take Michael back. And he says he should have tried to understand you more. He should have realised that you were just a lonely kid who didn't get on with her family. It's not unheard of for girls like that to go on the game. Though, of course, being Daniel, he thinks they should have more self-control.'

'I'm surprised he wants Angela to have Michael back though,' said Mary, then stopped, suddenly embarrassed.

'Oh don't worry, Mick knows that in a weak moment I let him seduce me. But I was very drunk and can't remember anything about it,' Janey said, winking.

Mary looked at her watch.

'We'd better go,' said Janey. 'Look I'll write down my address and number. And we'll send you a wedding invitation.'

'I remember. A footy stadium, wasn't it?' said Mary.

'That's right,' said Mick. 'You make sure you come. And

141

wear whatever you like, girl. And you don't have to bring the old geezer, I mean neither of the old geezers.' He winked at her.

'Mary,' said Janey, 'If you can get Daniel Hansen to my wedding then you aren't just a nun, you're a saint. Tell him he's invited too.'

23

Mary decided to tell Daniel that Janey had been to see her. It would be better than him finding out later. But what about her fling in Rome with Simon? She could not tell Daniel about that. At least not yet. She was annoyed that she had to think like that. That she still had be on her guard about doing the wrong thing and being found out. But what else can I do? She was arguing with herself all the way back to the shop. Fearing Daniel would be there and afraid that he would not. Suppose he's changed his mind? She didn't care any more whether it was love or need. She wanted him.

He was standing with his back to her. The first thing she saw was that wonderful white hair. And she wanted him. She could feel his body, feel him inside her. She remembered his voice, the things he would say when he made love to her; silly old-fashioned things, she had thought then.

But now her need for him made her despise herself. Why did she want someone who could be so cruel, who could look at her and call her such foul names? She stood looking at him, at the defensive shoulders. He was a stubborn man, he would always have to be right about everything, and she wanted him.

He was talking to Norman, who beamed when he saw Mary. Daniel turned with a blank expression.

'What would you like to do?' said Mary nervously. 'Have you had lunch?'

'Don't you have an apartment nearby?' he said coldly.

'Yes,' she said and turned to walk out of the shop, turning back to say goodbye to Norman. 'Please tell Hartley if he calls that I've gone home.'

Daniel followed her out of the shop. 'Are all your acquaintances homosexual, Mary?' he said sarcastically.

'Yes, every one of them,' she replied angrily. 'I would have thought you would be pleased.'

They arrived at Mary's flat in silence.

'I don't want to argue with you,' said Daniel. 'I want to know what your plans are.'

Mary tried to sound businesslike. 'Hartley is ill and cannot run the business. Norman and Barry are both getting old, so that only leaves me. We need someone to go to auctions and sales and do the buying. I also have to deal with the sale of Hartley's family home in Norfolk.' She stopped and looked at him. If only he would smile at her, anything but that cold expression. 'Oh yes, and I have just seen Janey. She called me to say she would be in London for the day and we met for lunch.'

'You must have had a lot to talk about,' said Daniel, without bothering to disguise the contempt in his voice.

'She's planning to get married. She introduced me to her fiancé and invited me to the wedding.'

'I see.' Daniel sat down suddenly. 'Mary, what are we going to do about our marriage? I have said I want us to try again. I know I should have tried to understand you. But you still continue to associate with your former . . .' He could not bring himself to say the word.

'Daniel, I can't go back to my family. Hartley has become like family to me. He looked after me. There was never any question of going back to my former life with him. I left that life before I returned to England the first time, some months before I met you. It was Hartley's idea that I become a nanny. And I was a good nanny, you witnessed this yourself. It's ironic that this man you appear to despise cared more about my feelings once he got to know me well than you did. And I hate having to explain myself to you.'

'Then why do you?'

'Why should I have to? You saw me in New York. I was good enough to look after Martha and Dan until my past surfaced. I am no different now. I was no different when I was sixteen

144

when I got into prostitution. I just had nowhere to turn. Hartley was the only friend I had.'

'Friend? How could you call such a monster a friend?'

'You must meet him. You'll see he's not a monster.'

'I intend to meet him. I have a lot to say to him.'

'Please, Daniel, he's ill now. And he has lost his partner. Anton died recently and Hartley is still grieving.'

'His partner? What do you mean?'

'He and Anton were together for seven years. They loved each other.'

Daniel suddenly hooted with laughter. 'Oh Christ. They loved each other!' He continued to laugh. Mary could not tell if he was amused or if this was an angry or bitter laughter. She could not bear the tension. She wanted a drink. But she had poured all the alcohol down the toilet. She went into the kitchen to make some coffee. She began to cry softly. She did not hear Daniel come into the room. She felt his arms around her.

'I'm sorry my darling,' he said. 'What can I do? I made a lot of mistakes. I will try to be nice to your Hartley. I will help you with the business. But right now I want very much to make love to you.'

If Mary had expected Daniel just to help out, she soon learned she was being naive. He said the only way he would do anything for Hartley would be if he could buy the business, or at least shares in it. Mary was horrified on Hartley's behalf. 'Please don't mention that to him while he's so ill, darling,' she said. 'He ran this business with Anton. We can't do that to him, please darling.'

'We cannot afford to be sentimental,' said Daniel. 'I'll put it to him,'

Mary tried to stay silent. But then she knew she could not let this go. 'No, Daniel, please don't, not yet. I mean it. Hartley is very vulnerable at the moment. By all means talk to him about how we can get someone to do the buying, but please, please don't try to take the business from him so soon.' Daniel was very reluctant to agree. All Mary could do was to get him to put off the meeting with Hartley. She called the doctor to come and see him. He thought it likely that losing both Anton and his mother could have worsened his heart condition. 'He could appear to get better. He could even have episodes of appearing to be well. But his heart could give out at any time. I'll leave you a prescription.' As he left the doctor added, 'I've talked to him about the possibility of surgery, Miss Palmer, but he was against it. It could just be a matter of time. I can arrange a nurse?'

'No, I can look after him,' she said.

In the meantime she and Daniel went, as they had arranged, to Norfolk to stay in Hartley's house and deal with the estate agents. She had been reluctant to leave Hartley but he said he was fine. She made Barry and Norman promise to call her immediately if anything happened. They said she was just a silly girl. Hartley was a young man and would see them off at least, and they had no intention of going for a while yet.

Hartley told Mary that having met Daniel and seen what Mary called his 'business face', for the first time in his life he was sorry for estate agents. But Mary and Daniel had a lot of fun, showing people around and finally choosing the best purchaser.

'While we're here,' said Mary, 'let's go to some auctions and get Hartley some new stock.'

'And while we're here, why don't we look for a house for ourselves?' said Daniel.

But Mary could not think about buying a house. She was increasingly worried about Hartley. And she was angry with Daniel for being on the make. For the next two months Mary fought Daniel over Hartley. Daniel railed at her in vain. 'Why are you protecting him? He raped you and put you on the game! You were just another tart to him. Why are you so sentimental? To him you were just a common whore!'

'Like I was to you, my darling, until you knew better,' replied Mary. 'Why do you have to be so nasty about prostitutes anyway? How many prostitutes have you known?'

Daniel said nothing and Mary started to laugh at him. But then she saw his face. 'Oh. You mean you have?'

'When Alicia was ill,' said Daniel. 'I did use prostitutes.'

'Use them,' said Mary. 'Is that what you really mean? Use them?'

'Well, yes, I suppose it is. I suppose I did use them.'

Mary looked horrified and it annoyed him. 'Yes, what else were they for? I was angry. I knew Alicia was not happy even before she became ill. She wanted to be a lawyer. I'm sure you've heard this already, I know Barbara is a gossip. She wanted to be a lawyer. I wanted a wife and children. I wanted a son. After Lauren was born, she said she wanted no more children. She refused to have any more. She had herself sterilised. I told her that was an act of wicked self abuse. She never felt the same about me again. Later, when the girls were married, she tried to get back into law but she got ill. She was very ill for four years with cancer. And then she died.'

'And you took out your anger on prostitutes, you used them,' said Mary. 'And you're only telling me this because you think I might know already. You're no better than me. You're a hypocrite, Daniel. I will never let you take the business from Hartley.'

They bought a large apartment in Half Moon Street, just around the corner from the shop, and at Mary's insistence Hartley came to live with them. She loved looking after him; cooking him 'sensible food' that would be kind to his heart or going with him on occasional outings to the cinema or a walk in Hyde Park. She spent hours reading to him. He became very forgetful and at times did not know who she was; sometimes he would call her 'mummy' which amused her.

She was happy to run the business while Daniel increasingly based himself in Norfolk and took over all the buying and selling at auctions. He became very successful at it and frequently travelled home to do business in the States. The business was booming. Whilst in New York he stayed with Angela and the kids. He did not tell Mary that Angela was urging him to make that stay permanent.

Mary knew they were drifting apart and she was angry with

147

him. She did not know how to talk to him about it. She was afraid of his anger but she was more afraid of her own.

Hartley had occasional lucid days. He told Mary, 'Don't neglect your husband for me, baby. I know he's not perfect. I know you think he's hard, but he's an empire builder. He can't help it. That's the way he is. Don't spend all your time with me.'

A couple of days later he died in his sleep of heart failure. Mary called Daniel to tell him and to say she would be arranging the funeral for the following Wednesday.

Daniel was cool. But he said he would come. 'Did he leave a will, Mary?'

'That's typical of you, Daniel. Well, I'm sorry but I'm too upset about this to look for it. I'm sure you would do a better job.'

Daniel put the phone down.

The funeral was to be in Hartley's home village in Norfolk. Mary called Daniel to tell him. 'It'll be easy for you to get there. It's only five miles from your house,' she said.

Daniel said he would try his best to be there. 'Let me know if you need anything, Mary,' he said.

Barry and Norman chose the hymns. Barry told Mary they wanted 'Butch, noisy hymns to wake the old bugger up.' They chose '*Bread of Heaven*' and *Onward Christian Soldiers*'.

'We want a good shout, Mary,' said Norman. 'We also thought of *Ravel's "Bolero"*. Hartley and Anton loved that.'

'No, I don't think so,' said Mary. 'That's too outlandish for the sticks.'

'Okay, baby, we'll save it for his wake,' said Barry.

Mary invited everyone she could think of. She wanted to fill the church with people and flowers. Hartley was to be buried alongside his mother and father. She tried to trace his brother Christopher but it proved impossible.

Mary sat in the front row with Barry and Norman, who held hands. Norman took Mary's hand with his free one as she looked around the church. She was pleased to see that Simon was there, sitting near the back. Mary gripped Norman's hand. She was determined not to cry. But it was no good. The

148

vicar had got to know Anton and Hartley in recent months and was picking his way gingerly through his sermon.

He's avoiding all reference to original sin for once,' said Barry in a loud stage whisper. 'So he'll not make it to sodomy and gonorrhoea, we have that to be thankful for.' Mary managed a smile and immediately felt the tears coming. She bit her lip but it did no good. She bit harder into her lip, so hard that it tore and bled. And then she was sobbing. Norman put his arm around her and she sobbed on his chest. She was feeling her loss and grief like a physical pain. She was sad about Hartley's illness and grief and she was missing him. She was afraid that she would not be able to manage the business without him; that Barry and Norman would die and she would let her beloved Hartley down. She was convinced that she was destined to fail him.

But it was the nine-year-old Mary, who had shed no tears at her father's death, who had said no goodbyes and who had paid no last respects, who sobbed uncontrollably. It was the lonely little girl who had played no part in her father's funeral who wept in the arms of an elderly homosexual. She was glad by then that Daniel had not come.

'So, what did Hartley the dastardly seducer do to deserve this devotion from you?'

'I don't know, Simon. He had no family left that I could find. His mum had died and he had not spoken to his brother for years. I couldn't trace Christopher, his brother. He's retired and apparently gone to live in France. I tried but I couldn't trace him there, either. I'm the only family at Hartley's funeral. I wasn't given the opportunity to go to my father's funeral. What I did for Hartley, though I loved him, too, was for my father.'

You're a funny girl,' said Simon. 'Perhaps you'll grow up one day. You behave like a child but listening to you, you're old before your time. It speaks of a lonely childhood with no companions but books.'

'I can feel another crack at my poor old Mum coming,' said Mary. But Simon just laughed.

'Did you go and see your family after all?'

'No. In the end I didn't go. I've had too much to do just lately. Maybe later. But the need to see them is receding. Marty wouldn't know me anyway and it would just confuse him. But I feel I've laid my father to rest in a way, through knowing Hartley.'

'Don't start that again,' said Simon impatiently. 'Do you know what you're saying?'

'Yes,' said Mary. 'I know what I'm saying.'

'But what about your marriage? What about your wonderful Daniel? Has he left you?'

'I expect he'll turn up when all the legal stuff starts,' said Mary. 'But it could be difficult. I'm not sure if Hartley left a will. If Daniel does come back I'll let him deal with it. He's been itching to get his hands on this business, anyway.'

Daniel arrived at Half Moon Street a week later but by that time Mary was emotionally drained. They hardly spoke to each other while Daniel sorted out Hartley's legal affairs. They were quite straightforward. He had left everything to Mary Palmer.

24

'So now we think the worst about each other, where do we go from here?'

'Mary, I don't think the worst of you. I've told you that I've tried to understand why you lived the way you did. All I ask is that you do the same for me.'

'Hartley called you an empire builder. He was right wasn't he, and he barely knew you. I know how you felt about him. But he told me to spend more time with you. He said I might lose you if I didn't.'

'Well I thought about leaving you Mary. When you insisted on him living in our apartment I seriously considered it. You and he were special to each other, I could see that, but I couldn't understand it. I was jealous, I suppose. He made that will leaving everything to you some time ago, when his . . . when Anton died. At least no one could call you a gold-digger this time.'

'Do you still love me, Daniel? Because if you really do then maybe we have a chance. If you can really accept me as I am.'

'Oh for Christ's sake, Mary. What do you expect of me? Of course I don't like everything about you, no one does about anyone, if they're honest. No one even likes everything about themselves. You can be very irritating and self-obsessed. And a bit holier than thou, which drives me mad.'

'Well if that means you do love me, then I think we should be all right. And if you do love me there is something you could do for me.'

'What's that?'

'No, wrong answer, Daniel you're supposed to say "Anything".'

151

'OK, you witch. Anything.'

'You promise?'

'Yes, I promise,' he said, laughing. 'I'll do anything.'

'Great. It's Janey and Mick's wedding in two weeks. And we are going.'

'That girl wrecked my daughter's marriage!' said Daniel.

'No, not on her own she didn't, and you said that yourself. You once said she had a good heart.'

'Let me think about it,' said Daniel.

'But I must reply soon and I would like to say we are both going. Look Daniel, I know this might seem hard. But Angela could have Michael back at any time, couldn't she? She can't help it if she is as stubborn as her old dad.'

'Come here, Mary,' he said. She came and put her arms around his neck. 'Why did you marry me?'

'I agreed to marry you because I was desperate. I didn't want to come back to England. I liked you and respected you but I had no sexual feelings for you. And then, during the ceremony, when I forgot my name, do you remember? You winked at me.'

Daniel winked. 'What, like this?' he said, laughing.

'Yes, you winked at me, to reassure me, I suppose. But I felt a sudden sexual charge. It was then I knew I did have feelings for you. It may seem strange now but I hadn't thought of you sexually before that moment. It all happened too quickly. I still thought of you as a kindly man, but the father of my employer.'

'And from the time I'd met you I found it hard to keep my hands off you,' said Daniel.

'You didn't,' said Mary. 'You never told me.'

'And now,' said Daniel, 'do you like sex with me?'

'The first time you made love to me *was* the first time. No one had made *love* to me before. I remember thinking at the time. You are a wonderful lover Daniel. But what about me? Do you like sex with me or are you always thinking of my past?'

'Well, no, I don't, because I had a year of wonderful sex

152

with you before I knew about the past. And when we got back together . . . no, I didn't think about it.'

'It doesn't sound as if you ever made love to a prostitute anyway, if you were simply engaged in dumping your anger on them.'

'So we worry too much about it instead of doing it,' he said. He kissed her mouth and then began to unbutton her dress. 'Come to bed with me now, my darling wife,' he said. 'And we can go to a wedding every week if that's what you want.'

25

'Will I ever be able to go and see Angela and the children, with you, of course, not by myself.'

'I won't say never. But not right now, darling,' Daniel said. 'She's putting a brave face on things, but I know underneath she's very unhappy.'

'Does she talk to Michael at all?'

'She seems to think she is being strong by keeping away from him. Martha and Dan see him, of course, he takes them out every Sunday but, oh it's a sad mess, Mary. They're not happy kids. They try for Angela's sake but they're torn in half.'

'They've lost their dad,' said Mary. 'It's very hard to get over. Look at me. I wasn't normal. I never had any boyfriends at all until I met you. For a long time you were like a father in my eyes. I admired Angela so much. I wanted to be like her. And I wanted a father like hers. And then her father became a knight in shining armour and rescued me. And he totally confused everything by insisting on marrying me.'

'But you don't see me as a father figure now, do you darling? I hope not. It doesn't sound healthy.'

'But you do look after me. And you are thirty years older than me. In some ways . . . She stopped, afraid to go on, not wanting to think too deeply about her attraction to Daniel and her need for him.

'What is it darling?' he said. He sounded worried. She wondered how much he had been worrying about it. She knew he blamed himself for Michael's problem and for the break-up of his favourite daughter's marriage.

'I love you Daniel, you know that, you're the best. I couldn't want for more. But you will leave me, like my Father did.'

'I will never leave you again, darling, you must believe me.'

He seemed so hurt, Mary began to cry. But she was angry with him. He was so full of self-assurance. Did he think he was immortal? She screamed at him: 'But you'll *die*, you fool, you'll die and leave me.'

He took her in his arms. 'Then we must have children darling,' he said. 'Then we'll be a family. And you'll have a family when I'm gone. And grandchildren. You won't be on your own.'

Daniel was thrilled when two months later Mary's pregnancy was confirmed.

'Everything will be fine now,' he told Angela on the phone. 'Mary will settle down now. She'll get over this fear of giving birth.'

'But you said she was hysterical all the time,' said his daughter.

'She's fine,' insisted her father.

'I suppose you're hoping for a son?' said Angela bitterly. 'But be careful, he may take after your wife, so you had better leave him well provided for.'

'I know I've hurt you, chicken, and I'm sorry,' said Daniel. 'Please see Mary, she has always admired you, she never wanted to cause you any pain.'

'Dad, you are a fool,' said his daughter. 'All Mary wanted was a substitute father to look after her. She's incapable of earning her own living. You'll be sorry you married her. Believe me. And I'll have nothing to do with her children. If you leave them anything, I'll contest the will.'

Mary sat looking at herself in the mirror. The image was blurred. She had heard that vodka was undetectable on the breath. Drinking helped her to cope with the feelings she did not understand about herself.

155

She had been having the dream again. She dreamed that she woke up and Daniel was there. But sometimes it was her father who was there. Her father who was saying he loved her. She was afraid. She became withdrawn. She could not bear to be with her thoughts.

If it wasn't for the baby she could stay with Daniel and it would be all right. She would look after him the way she had looked after Hartley. But she could not have the baby. It was wrong, it was disgusting to have the baby.

The nurse was looking at Mary with concern edged with contempt. The contempt was creeping into her voice as she spoke: 'You're nearly three months pregnant. This is a dangerous time to talk of an abortion. You haven't given the doctor a good enough reason. Why not have the child and put it up for adoption?'

'I can't, said Mary. 'I can't have my father's child.'